FINDING INERTIA

Nathan R. Yehle

For Laurie.

Table of Contents

Prologue

Alright, my friend, I've put this off for long enough.

I suppose it's time.

Thank you for the journal. I think about you every day.

My name is Inertia Hollins. Yes, that's my given name. My friends call me Ersch. This is a story about searching—for meaning, for connection, for ourselves—a story about the human experience of fleeting moments and enduring truths that we piece together and call our lives.

We are deeply imperfect creatures, despite all our efforts to appear to the contrary. Acknowledging that is a humbling experience. One I faced repeatedly. Although, amid our flawed and messy lives is our capacity to grow, and therein lies our real power. Like Sir Edmund Hilary said about Everest, "It is not the mountain we conquer, but ourselves." I certainly had a lot to conquer, and I suspect I'm not alone.

Some remarkable people entered my life along the journey and helped me in ways I'm unsure I could ever repay. Their stories are as important as mine. In a way, their stories *are my story.*

One of them once said that my struggle might become part of someone else's survival guide— a comment that I held on to and that eventually encouraged me to share the events of my life. While deeply personal, they seem universal enough that others may find comfort or inspiration in their telling. So, here I am, recalling the people, places, and moments that influenced me and the lessons I learned along the way. Perhaps the greatest lesson was that the value was already in the clay.

It just needed to be shaped.

CHAPTER ONE

Pay and Benefits

The door to my bedroom burst open, and the first sounds that cracked across my ears were, "Ersch! Get up! You're gonna be late!"

My tired, muffled voice replied from under my pillow, "Charlie, it's Sunday! Late for what?!"

"Hate to break it to you, hero, but yesterday was Sunday. Remember? We had that lovely dinner, and you carried on about your big interview tomorrow? Well, guess what, sunshine? Tomorrow has arrived, and by my estimate, you've got about twenty minutes to make it six blocks, or you're gonna miss your train."

That was Charlie. We met freshman year in high school, and he's had my back and been my best friend ever since—a detail he loves to remind me about. However, the realization that he was right filled me with the same shock as being pushed into a lake in springtime.

I gasped and threw my pillow against the wall. "Crap! That *was* yesterday!!!"

I sprung up out of bed like a bobber released from underwater. The covers made a wide arc across the room as I frantically dove into my suit and tie. Rushing into the kitchen, I was greeted by my oldest friend, sitting at our kitchen table in his bathrobe, eating his breakfast. He had the good fortune of working from home doing content creation for the podcast he founded back in college. His foolish grin was dripping with I-told-you-sos, but he refrained from teasing me, at least for the moment.

I crammed a piece of fruit in my pocket and a slice of toast from Charlie's plate in my mouth, and I was out the door. I could hear him howling with laughter as I bounded down the stairs and out the front of our building. As I broke out onto the sidewalk, I heard him call from the third-floor window, "Run, Inertia Hollins! Run!"

My dress shoes were not designed for sprinting, and as they clattered down the city streets, I could feel the blisters forming on my pinky toes. Six blocks later, I managed to hurdle over the metro turnstiles while scanning my commuter card in a manner worthy of an action hero movie as I barely slid through the subway doors just as they were closing. As I caught the handrail and my breath, the train slowly departed. I chuckled quietly to myself while picking little bits of toast off the roof of my mouth. What a ridiculous start to the day.

The train was precisely on time. A typical day on the C— dull, cramped, full of long faces lost in their phones or in whatever was playing through their earbuds. It shuffled us all off to our destinations and never complained. The rhythmic "tut-klack tut-klack" of the train always felt like the pulse of the city to me. The crush of people, the hurrying and urgency, and the perpetual motion felt like fluid coursing through the veins of a sleeping giant.

I desperately needed this job. For years, I'd been barely scraping by to get the credentials needed to work in the financial securities world, all the while surviving off the generosity of my well-to-do best friend. It made me feel ashamed, like I couldn't make it on my own, like I was less-than. It was a terrible feeling, being constantly beholden to someone else's support. My story was like most people's, a constant struggle to eke out a living in an increasingly expensive world. I longed for a little breathing room. I didn't need ultra-wealth; I just wanted to read from the left side of the menu and pick what I liked instead of reading from the right side to see what I could afford.

Charlie, like many of our friends, was a person of means—both earned and given. He would cover for me without hesitation if I couldn't make the rent or was unable to pay for something. He never let the finances get in the way, but his generosity felt very patronizing sometimes. It was hard on my self-worth to constantly feel like his charity case.

However, today was the chance to change all that. My destination was a few blocks away from the Chambers Street stop—a tall, daunting building so high I could barely see the top of it. I entered a large, bright, glass-walled atrium full of elevators and hustling professionals in expensive suits all rushing to their morning meetings.

I rode the elevator to the twenty-second floor with a friendly woman in a blue pantsuit. She had the warm, tired eyes of a kindergarten teacher and seemed to sense my nervousness.

"First day?" she offered kindly, breaking the silence.

"Interview, actually."

"Oh, really? Well, good luck, then," she replied.

"Thanks. Do you mind if ask—do you like working here?"

She hesitated a bit, cracked a warm smile, and said, "The pay is good, and they have great benefits."

Her response was interesting. It almost felt rehearsed. The elevator filled with silence again, and I couldn't help but try and dig a little deeper.

"You didn't answer the question," I said.

She paused briefly, seeming to consider my brashness as the elevator chimed at her floor. That kind smile crept back across her face as she exited the elevator, turned to me, and said, "You'll fit in just fine around here."

The doors closed, and I continued to ascend to my destination, struck by the odd exchange. Three floors later, the broad metal doors parted once again, and I was greeted by a large bronze lion. He looked like a gatekeeper to whatever lay beyond.

Here we go, I thought to myself as I approached the receptionist.

The young man behind the counter looked up from his computer only briefly and then continued typing as he asked who I was here to see. My response raised his eyebrow slightly, and he waved a disinterested hand at the chairs to the left of his desk. I settled into one, suddenly hit with a wave of nervousness. It felt like everything was riding on this—my reputation, my finances, maybe even my friendships. However, that same tiny whisper of resolve that made me apply for this position in the first place told me to hold fast. This role was a good fit for me. Now I just needed to convince the company of that.

A deep voice called out to the receptionist, and I was led into a space that seemed strategically designed to intimidate and impress. My interviewer feigned modesty at my obvious look of awe at the opulence of our surroundings. The ceiling was tall and textured, flanked by glass on two sides that overlooked the lower Manhattan skyline. A wall of shelves filled with books, ornate awards, and keepsakes stood opposite the incredible view. The centerpiece of the room was a broad mahogany conference table that looked like it had been hewn from some ancient forest.

They certainly spared no expense on the conference room, I thought, scanning my surroundings.

A few other members of the organization entered through the door and settled into their designated seats. They were all exceptionally well groomed and well dressed. We exchanged introductions, and the questions began. Having already been to dozens of interviews like this, the strategy was immediately apparent. I wouldn't go so far as to call them cutthroat, but you could tell by their no-nonsense demeanors, tight creases, and square jaws that this group took their work very seriously. They were focused on competency and results, and they were here to thin the herd.

The questions were fast and complicated, designed to trip people up. Matching their intensity, despite being very uncomfortable about it, I tried to respond in a way that hid my uncertainty and desperation. Thankfully, fear and excitement look the same.

"Demonstrate to us how you'll be able to bring our clients above average returns," one of them asked.

"In my previous role I consistently delivered eleven percent over the market average without really caring about the work," I replied bluntly.

"So, you think you're a hot shot?" another responded quickly.

His question was not unexpected. In interviews, most traders tried to get under your skin because the job was high pressure, and they needed people who could tolerate the mental strain. They were looking to see if I would crack, but I had been down this road before.

I smiled calmly despite mountains of internal anxiety and said, "While I appreciate the title, no. I think I'm good with numbers and pattern recognition, and I think that's a hard skill to teach."

The interview carried on this way for a while, but my approach must have struck a chord with their team, because in no time we were all laughing and talking about things unrelated to the position. After about a half hour of friendly conversation, it seemed evident to me that no one else had really made it this far.

The hiring manager, my would-be future boss, was a stout and discerning middle-aged guy named Louis who had bushy eyebrows and a salt-and-pepper goatee. He shook my hand firmly with a broad grin as we concluded the interview. He was eager to book a follow-up meeting and seemed ready to talk compensation with me were it not for the other employees in the room.

I left their office with a spring in my step and a huge boost of confidence, practically punching the button on the elevator. The doors slid open, and I rode down with a sharp-dressed man seemingly in his mid-fifties. He nodded quickly, the obligatory New York hello, and then looked down at his phone. I let out a deep sigh of relief.

"Well, that sounded good," he said with a slight grin.

"Yeah," I replied. "I just had a great interview—I think I'm the person they're looking for."

"Congrats."

"Thanks. How long have you worked here?" I asked.

"Me? Well, going on twenty-eight years now. Got the job right out of college."

There was heaviness in his response. He stared at the wall of the elevator with a weary gaze. I asked what part of town he was from and attempted a few other pieces of small talk. There was a monotone complacency in his replies—maybe even a hint of regret.

I remembered the elevator ride earlier that morning and risked my question a second time. "Do you like working here?"

He tilted his head slightly and shrugged as he said, "The pay is good, and they have great benefits."

My eyes grew wide. The elevator opened, and he exited to his floor. I watched the doors close slowly. I rode down alone several more floors in silence before the doors opened to the wide glass atrium, now glowing with the afternoon sun.

I said aloud, "You didn't answer the question."

⬧⬧⬧⬧

I grabbed a late lunch at a falafel cart close to the subway entrance. The initial high from the interview was starting to wear off, and the train ride home was filled with mixed emotions. As I stood there hanging onto the handrail, my blistered toes reminded me that I probably overdid it on my a.m. sprint to the train. My mind, as usual, was a noisy room of competing voices. I wanted the position, but did I really? OK, I wanted the money the position would provide, and judging by the people I spoke to, the salary and fringe benefits were considerable.

So why was I so unsettled? If they offered me the job, would I seriously not take it based off the comments of a few passersby on my way in and out of the building? That seemed ridiculous, but I couldn't help but think that their comments were a warning. Here I was evaluating if this was a good fit for me after leaving the interview ecstatic. Was my heart really in this? Did my heart really need to be in it? Why did I need to be passionate about my job? Don't I deserve to do something I love? It was like a silent game of ping-pong in my mind. There were pros and cons on both sides and no clear decision.

The train loudspeaker chimed for the stop on 14th Street and shook me from my ponderings. Time to get back home. The six blocks from the train seemed to crawl by. The storm of competing thoughts rolling around in my head had me so caught up that I walked right past the entrance to our building. Realizing that I was at the end of the block and needed to backtrack, I chided myself for being so airheaded.

"What an idiot you are sometimes, Inertia," I said to myself as I climbed the stairs to our place. I had a bad habit back then of constantly talking down about myself. Charlie hated it. He would regularly remind me that my brain believed what I told it, so I should "be my own biggest cheerleader."

He always had some pearl of wisdom to share when I was down and a snarky comment when I was a little too prideful. While the advice was always appreciated, we were very different people. I preferred the quiet of my own space and the company of a few close friends, and I generally kept to myself. He was the biggest social butterfly imaginable. Charlie put the "E" in "Extra." Today was no exception. As I walked through the door to our apartment, his face lit up with a huge smile.

"Oh, and there he is—our aspiring Wall Street Wolf!" Charlie hopped up from his favorite reading spot, book in one hand while setting down one of those tiny espresso cups with the other. His face was full of anticipation. "My meeting with my media team was unusually short, and I was just enjoying a little chill time waiting for your return. And here you are! Glorious! Anyway, my next video is going to be pure cinema. I can't wait for you to see it! It should be live on the channel tonight. But I've carried on about myself quite enough. Tell me about your interview! I need all the tea, even the boring stuff. Don't skip anything. I'm assuming you crushed it?"

"Hi, Charlie," I replied, pulling off my suitcoat and throwing it over a chair, "Yeah, the interview went well. I think I'm their guy."

"Excellent! I asked my chat to send positive vibes out into the universe for you all day today. Clearly, they have worked, which is wonderful because that means I don't need to cancel the dinner reservations I made this morning. Come, come, get cleaned up—we're headed out to celebrate!"

"You made reservations to celebrate my new job after I left for the interview?"

"Child, you need to begin with the end in mind! Have I taught you nothing?!" Charlie said, slamming his book closed and tossing it back in his reading nook. "Besides, there's this new fusion place I want to try. I hear they make amazing sushi and wrap it in a burrito with other goodies. I'm paying, you're going, and that's the end of the discussion," he said with a wry smile.

I nodded, a little curious. My interest was piqued. I changed quickly, and we headed out. Charlie seemed to pick up on my internal distress on the walk there.

"So ... if the interview went so well, then why do you look like someone stole your lunch money? Oh my God! Were you mugged? You don't look mugged? Did something happen on the way home?"

I shrugged, not wanting to get into it. "Nah, nothing happened. Just a lot to consider."

"How long have we been friends? Huh? How long?"

I smiled. I knew what was coming. "I dunno, Charlie, *since forever?*"

"Forever and a day, Inertia Hollins! You think I don't know when something's bugging you?" he replied.

"Ah, I guess it's nothing, Charlie. I'm just stuck in my head like usual. The interview really did go great. It's a solid company with good pay and ..."

I stopped short, ashamed to finish the sentence. My heart sank a little. I hadn't even landed the job, and I already sounded like the people in the elevator.

"And?" Charlie continued, eyebrows raised and hands to his sides. "And what?"

"What if I hate it but make a ton of money? What if I really don't want to be a financial professional? What if I just applied because it will allow me to earn my keep? Is that worth the price of my joy?"

"Ah … and now we come to it," Charlie said with a knowing nod. "That's the reason for those heavy shoulders. Well, that question is older than both of us, I'm afraid. Do you love your work and hate the pay? Is the career what brings you joy? Or is the job just a tool, and you find your fulfillment at your kitchen table surrounded by your friends and loved ones?"

He clicked his tongue loudly. "Tough one, Ersch. Some people, granted not many of us, thrive in that high-powered career life. They live for bigger challenges and go off to build empires. A handful probably beat the odds too and have fulfilling lives and relationships outside of their work, but I bet most look back in regret at all the sacrifices they made for that corner office."

I nodded, considering what he was saying. For a guy in his early twenties, Charlie was wise beyond his years. I envied that. We were only six months apart in age, but it felt like decades of difference in life experience. Maybe that was an advantage of being more outgoing. Maybe he was just learning faster than me.

"I don't know, Ersch, it's easy to get wrapped up in the unhappy urgency of urban life. I saw it with my dad. Ugh, total workaholic, that man. Didn't leave any time for his family. That's why most people find something with low stress and average pay so they can maximize time with the people that count."

We walked in silence for about another block. He made some good points. However, I was still young and single and had plenty of time for things like that. My immediate need was to find a way to pull my weight, and this felt like my best chance, even if I was apprehensive.

Charlie smiled. "I think it'll be great for you. Why not grind out a few years to get some seed money for whatever else you'd rather do? But! And this is a big but. Like the saying goes, "Don't be so busy making a living that you forget to build a life.""

He stopped suddenly and raised his left arm like a game show host while opening a large ornate glass door with his right.

"Enough of that for now. The sushi burrito beckons, Inertia, and I am famished."

⧼⧽⧼⧽

A few days later I got the good news phone call from Louis. They wanted me for the job. At that point, enough time had passed that I had suppressed the mountain of self-doubt that sprung up after my interview. Louis's voice might as well have been a winning lottery ticket. I silently jumped around the apartment as he shared the details of the compensation package with me. I accepted on the spot, verbally of course, and perhaps that was a little naïve, but it was way more money than I had ever been offered before, so I leapt at the chance. A small shred of my own independence, finally!

The following Monday was my start date. This time I made sure my alarm was set so that another mad dash to the train wasn't necessary. When the elevator doors parted again, there was the big bronze lion at the front of the office. I affectionately named him Leonidas after the ancient Spartan king. My orientation lasted about a month, after which I officially started taking clients and performing for the company. It didn't take me long to fall into the swing of things.

Also, the people I met during my interview were correct. The compensation was excellent, but we earned every penny. The job gobbled up a ton of time. There were days I worked so late that it almost made sense to sleep in the office. Having such a demanding schedule meant that I started to miss out on some events with friends and needed to cancel a lot of plans. I was still in the process of "paying my dues," so I couldn't really take any time for myself. Most days, I would head into the office before sunrise and leave after dark. I had to remind myself regularly that the lack of free time was made up for by the salary. However, the lack of socialization with anyone other than my colleagues began to take its toll.

Don't get me wrong, I was very grateful to have the job. It was much easier to support myself, afford a few things, and have a little money in the bank. It certainly took away the stress of covering my share of our West Village apartment. It also made me feel a little more dignified. There's nothing wrong with being proud of your work, but if I'm honest, maybe I was a little too proud. No one at my office was curing cancer or saving lives. Really, we were just placing bets for the city's social elite. After about five months of the commute, the stress, and the time commitment, my enthusiasm started to wane. The shine of the position had worn off a bit, and Charlie's comment began to ring in my ears during my Monday morning strategy meetings.

"Don't be so busy making a living that you forget to build a life."

CHAPTER TWO

The First Law of Motion

It's probably time for a little backstory. Currently, I wear the unique-ness of my name like a badge, but in my early years, it did me no favors, and so I hid it like a scar. By typical standards, my name branded me an outsider, which made it hard to make friends and made me an easy target for mockery. Some kids can be very cruel—their identities aren't solidified, some are insecure, and some come from broken homes or have unhealed trauma. It's just easier to pick on the kid with the weird name than it is to face their own troubles.

Unfortunately, because of this, I was ridiculed a lot growing up. It made me incredibly self-conscious (something I'm still working on as an adult). Regretfully, I internalized almost all of it. I'm ashamed to admit that for a while I believed all the unkind things that people said about me.

I grew terrified of what the next person might say and tended to overthink everything. I would replay conversations in my mind and analyze how they could have gone better or, even worse, rehearse arguments that never happened just to be prepared in the event of conflict.

The lesson, obviously, was that most people didn't spend a second of their day thinking about me. Their focus was on themselves. That self-imposed cage of public opinion we build in our minds? Yeah, it's not real. It's made of thoughts—fickle, malleable, replaceable thoughts.

In hindsight, it feels silly to be so beholden to the opinion of others, but we're all human, and one of our greatest needs—second probably only to survival—is a need to belong. We want to fit in, be liked, and feel like we're part of something. Why else would we chase likes and follows on social media? Why do sports teams and musician fandoms exist? How about subscriberships, clubs, or conventions? Everyone wants to find their tribe. There's a sense of security in it. When you're surrounded by like-minded people, you can lower your guard. We crave sameness. We seek community. We long for it.

I certainly did. I had an overwhelming desire to be liked, but few people ever gave me a chance because they were quick to pick on me about my name. So, for a while, I was convinced that there wasn't a tribe for me and that maybe I'd never have someone to call "my person."

All of that changed when I met Charlie. It was my freshman year of high school, and my family had recently moved into the area. I was a new face in a new place with a weird name in the middle of the school year. Not the best start. It was a huge school, and the homerooms were cafeterias divided alphabetically. I sat alone at an empty table, and Charlie was the only person in the crowd brave enough to befriend the new kid.

"Charles Margolis the Third," he said with an outstretched hand. I looked up at this impeccably dressed, confident kid that looked a little younger than me with styled black hair and a broad smile. He had one of those gazes that would trap you and hold your attention.

"Uh, hi. I'm Inertia Hollins."

His handshake was firm but comforting. "Inertia? That's your real name?!" I nodded, expecting to be teased, like usual. "Well, Mr. & Mrs. Hollins must be very interesting people. First day, Inertia?"

Surprised at his response, I said the only thing that came to mind,

"Uh … yeah."

"Oy vey, and so eloquent too! Well, Inertia Hollins, don't worry those big, sad brown eyes of yours. It's a big school, but I run it, so you'll be well received by this sea of unwashed heathens."

"Thanks, Charles Mar … Margolis."

"Easy, kid. It's only three syllables. Also, call me Charlie," he said with a slick smile. "Everyone does."

He was right. In a school of over two thousand students, it seemed like everyone knew who Charlie was. Even upper-classmen and seniors. He was like the de facto prince of high school. I had no idea how he knew so many people, let alone remembered all their names. He was like a search engine for his little corner of the world. Charlie had details on everyone. He's the one that first gave me my nickname.

"We've got to come up with something better than Inertia," he said one day at lunch. "It's too long."

"Better? What do you mean? That's my name."

"It's too long," he repeated.

He sounded my name out phonetically, "In-er-shugh. Maybe Shugh? Nah, that sounds too much like Shaw, and he's a creeper." He sat there rubbing his chin for a second, when a smile broke across his face. "I've got it! Ersch. I'm gonna call you Ersch!"

"Ersch? How do you spell it?"

"I dunno, like it sounds. With an 'E' and a mush of consonants," he said with a shrug. "Spell it however you want, or don't spell it at all. I just think it's cool."

"Ersch?" I said it a few times in my head; each time, it sounded a little better than before. A nickname from the most popular kid at school? It wasn't a cheap shot at me either. He meant it genuinely. It was a good feeling, like a step toward being accepted.

"Alright, Charlie, I'll roll with it. Ersch it is."

Turns out, Charlie had a bit of a knack for this sort of thing. My nickname caught on fast. Soon, I wasn't just the weird new kid with an odd name; it was like I became this exotic animal. Everyone wanted to know more about me—mostly because of my friendship with Charlie. He was a fascinating person, completely obsessed with meeting the next face, getting to know the next person, like he had no limit for people's stories. I asked him about it once on the way home from school.

"How do you do that, Charlie?"

"Do what?" he replied with his signature raised eyebrow.

"Talk to anyone about anything at any time, and somehow, they love you for it, they never forget you, and they can't wait to see you again! If I attempted half the conversations you do, they'd laugh at me."

"That's because you're focused on the wrong thing, Ersch. You're looking at *you* and what people might think of *you*. Most people? They aren't thinking about you. They're thinking about themselves or how they can do life better. If you took your eyes off yourself for a second and dropped that wounded look you always carry around, you'd find that everyone is waiting for someone to notice them. The minute you do, and then pay them a little kindness, you're practically besties for life. It's like a drug. Really, I do it for selfish reasons."

"That's pretty wise, Charlie."

"Yeah, maybe I'll write a book someday."

"What would you call it?" I asked with a grin.

"Something catchy."

Venturing my own idea, I asked, "What about *Life Lessons by Charlie Margolis?*"

Charlie stopped dead in his tracks. "Good Lord, please don't ever say those words in that order again."

"Seriously?!" I chuckled, throwing my arm over his shoulder. "I think that's catchy enough."

He sneered, tilting his head in my direction. "Yeah, like bottom-shelf-of-the-self-help-section catchy. You're lucky I'm your friend, Inertia Hollins. Someone needs to save you from yourself."

∾∾∾

As for Charlie's story, his grandfather, Charles Margolis Sr., was the owner of very successful law firm that Charlie's father, Charles Margolis Jr., was the managing partner of. As you would expect, this meant incredibly long hours such that Chalie's mother, Julia, basically raised him on her own. When he was seventeen, his grandfather died in his sleep. Four months later, Charlie's dad passed suddenly from a heart attack, leaving the law firm leaderless. Their equity (which was considerable) passed directly to Charlie and his mother.

Wanting nothing to do with the firm after her husband's death, Julia sold all her shares to the new managing partners and invested the proceeds. Charlie did the same. I was never told the full amount, but it must have been significant because Julia and Charlie lived an upper-middle class NYC lifestyle off the interest alone.

Also, Charlie never wrote a book, but about three months into our sophomore year of college, he started a food, fashion, and city-living podcast called *Metropcicle*. In roughly a year, he had over a million subscribers. Between the ad revenue from his podcast and other socials, plus his investments, Charlie lived very well.

I was not so fortunate. My life was earned through long hours at an assortment of jobs throughout my college years and early adulthood. I envied Charlie's independence, but what he did felt like something that only extroverts were suited for, and that seemed beyond my reach at the time. Not that I didn't have a desire to be more outgoing, but my fear of public opinion was just too strong for me to take any action. So, I lived my life as a quiet observer. However, there were still a lot of benefits to being Charlie's best friend. One of the biggest was meeting two amazing people that became some of my closest friends, second only to Charlie himself.

⊰⊱⊰⊱

The night before my big interview at Louis's investment firm, we were invited to a late summer gathering at what many would consider the ideal living arrangement for a city-dweller. We're talking a fifth story, top floor, corner loft apartment with high ceilings and a rooftop patio. It felt like the set of a movie or a sitcom. It was a small event, only twenty people or so. I was appreciating a beautiful summer sunset over the city skyline when my ever-animated friend approached with two women at his side.

"Inertia Hollins, I'd like you to meet our hosts for this fine event, Alicia D'Archangelis and her lovely wife Samm Kendricks." He gestured to me with a flourish of his hands.

"Ladies, this is my very best friend in the whole world, Inertia Hollins."

Alicia was average height with fiery burgundy curls and piercing hazel eyes. She was incredibly well dressed and carried herself with confidence and sophistication, but I detected none of the arrogance that some of the social elites were known for. On the contrary, her smile was warm and inviting, but there was an air about her that commanded respect. Still waters run deep, as the saying goes.

"So, this is the famous Inertia we've heard so much about," she said with an extended hand. "A pleasure to meet you." I extended my hand to meet hers, but as soon as our palms touched, Alicia pulled me in for a hug. This wasn't one of those weak socialite embraces either. She was strong and squeezed me like a sibling. "We've been fans of *Metropcicle* since Charlie's first episode. He speaks very highly of you on his podcast. I'm glad we could finally meet."

I had a terrible habit back then of not believing the good that others said about me. An insecurity from my childhood that was hard to shake. Funny how it's so easy to believe the bad things we think about ourselves but so hard to accept the good that others say about us. So, when Alicia paid me her compliment, I dismissed it almost reflexively, shaking my head to let her know I wasn't all that special.

In contrast to Alicia, her wife Samm was bubbly and sociable, with wavy blonde hair that she wore pulled back in a messy bun. She had these big, deep, chocolate brown eyes and was dressed much more casually than Alicia. Samm seemed to be the louder, more chaotic member of the duo. She quickly dispensed with any social decorum for her authentic self. She was about the same height and build as Alicia, and she gave me just as strong of a hug.

"Hi! I'm Samm!" she said with a quick giggle.

"Sam? Like, short for Samantha?" I asked.

"No, just Samm."

"Like, S-A-M?"

"No, two Ms," she replied.

"Two Ms? That's odd."

She laughed. "Says the guy who got his name from science class."

Charlie threw his hands to the side and shook his head. "In thirty seconds, you manage to embarrass me and offend our hosts!"

Samm was quick to assure us that she was just messing with me, and she hadn't taken any offense. I could feel my face flush and apologized for my rudeness. She gave me a wink and a quick punch on the arm, and all was forgotten.

"So, what do you do for work, Inertia?" Samm asked.

"Me? I work in commodities and securities trading. I have an interview with a pretty big firm tomorrow, in fact. Could be the break I've been looking for. Seems like the place would be a big boost for my career," I replied.

"No kidding! A real-life finance bro! Well, good luck. I hope they let you keep your soul," she said with a smirk.

I laughed uncomfortably, trying to mask my uneasiness.

"What do you guys do for a living?" I asked.

Charlie jumped in. "These two fine specimens are the lead aerial performing artists for a world-renowned circus troupe. Tickets for their next show are basically the hottest item in the whole city right now. It would be easier to have lunch with Ghandi at this point."

I didn't understand what that meant, but it sounded interesting.

"Like, flying trapeze or human cannonball type stuff?" I asked apprehensively.

"Not exactly," Alicia said and smiled broadly. "We have a pair of extra tickets if you two would like to come see for yourselves?"

I was immediately dismissive. The circus wasn't my thing. All I could think of were creepy clowns and abused animals. Charlie, conversely, lit up like Times Square.

"You bet your life we'll take them! Girl, your show has been sold out for months!" he exclaimed.

I looked over at him anxiously. More guests arrived, and our hosts stepped away to greet them. My immediate reaction was to tell Charlie all the reasons that I thought it was a bad idea, including not being seen at a show like that. There was a level of professionalism I felt I needed to maintain. I said as much to Charlie, unaware that I was still in earshot of Alicia.

"Well, Mr. Margolis, your friend holds us in such high esteem," Alicia said. Looking at me with a forgiving smirk, she continued, "I understand your apprehension, Inertia. Most Wall Street types don't gravitate to the arts, but I think you'll be pleasantly surprised if you attend. Provided, of course"—she let out a small laugh— "your would-be employer lets you off your leash for an evening."

I looked down at the ground, wishing it would open and swallow me whole. I used to do that to myself a lot. I would express my apprehension about something I knew little about and embarrass myself or expose some underlying insecurity.

Samm overheard Alicia tease me and rejoined the three of us. "Oh, now you've done it," she said with a laugh. "Now you've got to come, Inertia. Please? Promise you'll come. I swear you'll have a good time. Please? *Please!?*"

Sensing that she wasn't going to give up easily, I nodded and said, "OK, fine, I promise I'll go."

Samm bounced in place and let out a short squeal. "Eeeee! You won't be disappointed. It's gonna be awesome!"

As the party died down, the four of us sat around their patio and talked for several more hours. It was amazing how quickly we all became friends. It was almost like we were a lost family, finally reunited. It was so easy to be myself around them; everything clicked. It just felt right.

Before we left, Samm threw one arm over Charlie's shoulder and the other over mine. Alicia did the same, and we formed a small huddle of sorts. We said our farewells for the evening in our little friend circle. At the time, I had no idea how necessary their friendships would become, how much hardship they would help me through, or the catalysts that all three of them would become in my life.

CHAPTER THREE

Coerced into Wonder

"I'm not a curmudgeon … What does that even mean?"

Charlie's left eyebrow raised slightly as he tilted his head and let out a curt "Ha!"

"It means you're terribly boring, my dear Inertia, and if you don't come with me tonight—like you promised—then Samm and Alicia will stop inviting us to their fantastic social gatherings, and I will be forced to find a new best friend that is several grades more outgoing than the last."

About six weeks had passed since the party. I was still in the thick of my probationary period at the new job and barely had time to breathe. The ladies' performance was that night, and I was trying to get out of it. Charlie stood there, glaring at me with pursed lips and hands on his hips as I crafted an argument about how tired I was. I could tell by the look on his face about halfway into my loosely formed excuses that he was having none of it.

"Inertia, just say yes."

"It's a bad idea, Charlie. I've got to get up super early tomorrow so I can get in before the rest of the team. I'm still the rookie in the office."

"Oh my God, it's one night! They aren't going to fire you if you aren't super early. This is important."

"So is my job! I don't have the luxury of a golden parachute like you do. I don't come from money. I need to work to pay my bills!"

"Excuse me?!"

I wanted to reach into the air and un-speak the words. I knew I'd messed up.

"Golden parachute?!" he was shouting now. "My father is dead, Inertia! He's dead! I'll never hear his voice again, never see his face, never hear his laugh or hear him say he's proud of me! You can call your dad right now and have everything *I can't!* Don't you dare use that as an excuse! You think money is a fair trade for his life?! You think I wouldn't give up every penny for more time with him?!"

I winced, saddled with immediate regret. "You're right. I'm sorry, that was mean. You didn't deserve that."

He sighed. "Damn right I didn't! Now stop being such a schmuck and come to the show with me!"

"Can't you take your mom, or your editor, or anyone else but me? I really don't think I …"

He cut me off, clapping his hands with each word. "Inertia! Hollins! Just! Say! *YES!*"

I sighed, shaking my head. "Fine! I'll go, but I have appearances to maintain now, Charlie. I have, I don't know— professional standards! I can't screw this up. Besides, I'm a grown man now, and grown men don't go to the circus!"

I walked into the bathroom and slammed the door. His muffled voice sounded on the other side. "We're leaving in thirty minutes, and for the record, you're only twenty-five, Inertia. 'Grown men' live well into their eighties. And another thing"— he was shouting again— "with that attitude, you are not a man but a scared little boy that is so concerned with the opinions of others that he has made them his prison! Now hurry up!"

Ouch. I turned on the shower to that familiar hiss of falling water against the tile, pulled my shirt off, and stared at myself in the mirror. As usual, he was right, and his words laid me as bare as the pale skin and sad eyes that stared back at me from the mirror. However, that was the thing about Charlie. He made those statements in private and never to embarrass me. He accepted me for who I was, but he also cared enough to remind me that I could be more, even if he was a little mean about it.

The room slowly filled with steam as the image in the mirror became clouded and obscure. I wiped my hand across the glass and forced a smile. Talking to my reflection, I repeated his earlier comment, "Just say yes." *Maybe tonight will be fun*, I thought. I stepped into the shower.

What is it about a hot shower? Am I right? It may be the last great sanctuary for humankind. Something about hot water beating on my back has always put things in perspective for me. The wounds of my childhood resurfaced again. I leaned against the shower wall, letting the water fall over me. There was this pit of anxiety in my chest that I struggled to soothe. It felt like I was falling from someplace high up but couldn't find anything to grab ahold of. Balling up my fist, I punched the shower wall in frustration.

My reasoning was stupid. My boss wouldn't send the etiquette police to get me if I went to the show. Why did I make such a big deal out of this stuff? What was my problem? Why was I so concerned about some things but not about others? It didn't make sense. I shook my head, letting the water run off the front of my hair, staring at my feet and breathing in the steam. I gathered my resolve. My back straightened. I forced another smile. I said to myself, "Yeah, tonight will be fun."

I got dressed quickly in my favorite pair of faded straight-leg blue jeans and an oversized navy hoodie. If I was going to be dragged out to something I didn't want to go to, I was at least going to be comfortable. I was headed for the door when Charlie stopped me.

After a sharp, irritated inhale, he said, "Please tell me you aren't going out in that?!"

"What? What's wrong with jeans and a hoodie? And besides, we're going to a circus. A circus, Charlie … with smelly animals, peanuts, and strange people dressed in funny costumes."

He clicked his tongue and shook his head at me.

"This from the man that was so concerned about appearances that he wanted to stay home. This is not a typical circus, my dear uncultured friend. This is Cirque, with a Q, and it's far more refined than you think. I refuse to let you attend Alicia and Samm's show looking like that."

He wandered into his room, mumbling something under his breath about me being a Neanderthal. He returned a minute later with a blazer and matching button-down.

"For crying in the rain, here, wear this." He handed me the clothes. He then placed both hands firmly on my shoulders and gave me a warm smile. "Clothes make the man. So, dress like you own the bank, Inertia, not like you need a loan from one."

"Another *Life Lesson by Charlie Margolis*," I replied cynically. My eye roll was so exaggerated I'm sure it was audible, but I quickly changed. Charlie dressed sharp wherever he went. So much so that I often borrowed his clothes so that I didn't look like his assistant when we went out someplace nice. I had a few suits for work but hated wearing them outside the office. Charlie never missed a chance to look stylish.

The ride there was uneventful, typical summertime in the city. Loud music and car horns filled the air. People crowded the sidewalks on both sides, sitting on benches and doorsteps as others passed by. The streets were packed with traffic all stuck in the rhythmic compression of the stoplights. The smell of food was never far from your nose.

We arrived at a crowed arena with the steady hum of a thousand conversations, and I peered out at what looked like a pale single spotlight on a circular stage. We found our seats, and my curiosity started to build. Trying not to let on that I may have been anticipating our friends' performance, I armored myself with a little protective sarcasm and said, "Well, at least we're far enough back that we won't be able to smell the elephants."

Charlie struck me with his program booklet with a loud smack.

"Behave," he said with a grin. No sooner did I settle back down in my seat than the lights began to dim.

What a fool I was.

There were no elephants or peanuts here.

The performance started with calm blue and green light casting shadows over a meticulously crafted background that looked like forest, but from a nightmare. Soft, lonely music played as a vocalist in an elaborate white and blue dress reminiscent of the Victorian Renaissance occupied the lone spotlight and began to sing an aria. Her voice filled the room like a wave, meandering around us and saturating everything. I had no idea a human's voice could sound like that ... could ... *feel* like that. Every hair on my arms stood as I leaned forward in my chair.

A second spotlight appeared on the stage, blanketing a pair of performers in costumes of similar shades and colors, but this duo was in form-fitting clothing that displayed their impressive physiques. Gradually and deliberately, they began a series of intricate movements, the larger of the pair acting as a base and the smaller balancing along portions of the other's body.

They manipulated their arms and legs in impossible ways, slowly turning and gliding past one another like a delicate waltz, all the while suspended by the strength of one hand or one foot. They bent and stretched their appendages wide, freezing in holds like human statues that displayed their incredible strength as the beautiful vocalist blanketed the audience with her song. Every breath they took was synchronized; every movement of their bodies rippled muscles with quiet tension—an elegant display of balance and power. The conclusion of their act was a humble bow as the crowd applauded and the music changed, welcoming the next act.

A loathsome dirge gave entrance to a broad-shouldered man with deep ebony skin who exchanged silent pleasantries with the other cast members crowding the stage as he threw a single white ball into the air. One became two, and three, and then four. This new performer turned out to be an impeccable juggler—seven, eight, nine spheres thrown perfectly in the air as he spun and rolled about as if he had been born into the skill. At one point, his arms were moving so fast they seemed to disappear in the precision of each toss.

Tumblers and lighthearted clowns flooded the stage as the music shifted to a bright tune and an explosion of acrobatics and comedy that was met with rolling laughter and even more applause. A wiry young pair rolled out these large metal wheels that began spinning and gliding along the inside, arms and legs darting about like the particles of an atom. The night played on this way, act after act, and I found myself riveted in the otherworldly performance.

I was enjoying the show so much that I had completely forgotten we were here to see our friends. That's when all the lights in the arena went dark. The two solemn spotlights illuminated the floor as these thick red silks descended from the ceiling.

A soft chorus of women's voices complemented a calming melody as Samm and Alicia stepped into the light. Their hair pinned back tight with streaks of silver ribbon, faces adorned with jewels, and costumes that glistened in the pale spotlight. They bowed quickly to each other, their performance attire mirror opposites. Then they sprang into the thick crimson fabric, wrapping and turning, legs and arms purposefully flowing in perfect synchronicity.

As they climbed, bodies covered with wrapped red silk, they released hands and legs, stretching into incredible poses, suspended dozens of feet above the stage. They began to swing back and forth on the silks as the excess fabric opened below them into a long, ruby-colored trail. They drew closer to one another and then suddenly dove at each other, a single hand outstretched, locking wrists together and spinning out of the fabric as they rolled and pitched their bodies back down to the stage floor.

They grabbed the fabric and began to run in a large arc across the stage as the chorus grew louder, and without warning, Samm and Alicia leapt at the audience as the rigging of the silk raised them into the air above us. Sailing across the crowd in a broad flowing circle of red silk, they looked like angels, like Valkyries. There was an instant, and only that, when Samm and I locked eyes. It remains one of my most precious memories, even if it was only for a moment. The peace in her eyes was unquestionable. Indescribable. Complete. It struck me such that tears began to softly roll down my cheeks.

They completed their flight above the audience, landing on the stage floor, and began again to spin and climb into the fabric. The music grew quicker, the chorus louder still, and the pair climbed impossibly high into the air, balling up more of the red silk. At the crescendo of the music, they released their bodies, falling to the earth at a terrible speed as the crowd collectively gasped, stricken with fear and wonder as the pair plummeted to the stage. Gripping the silk at the precise instant, they stopped mere inches from the stage floor—backs arched and smiles beaming.

The crowd exploded into cheers and applause as the music slowed and the lights faded to black. The whole audience were on their feet howling adulations. I found myself sobbing like a fool, filled with an awe akin to Christmas morning. I almost passed up the chance to see this. I resolved to *just say yes* next time, whatever our next adventure was. It was a small but deeply meaningful point for me. I was typically very averse to anything outside my comfort zone.

We waited outside the performers' entrance for Samm and Alicia to emerge. Charlie, being the boisterous extrovert, dove at the two of them, circling them in his arms in a monstrous hug.

"That was amazing!" he exclaimed.

Samm asked cautiously, "You really liked it? Like, it wasn't too artsy for you guys?"

"Girl, you shut up, that was fantastic! You two were made for this!" he replied.

Alicia nudged my side and gave a warm, knowing glare. "Hello, Inertia, and what did you think of the show this evening?"

"Ally, I ..."

The words to describe how I felt were lost on me. "I had no idea … you both were … it was … it was wonderful."

"Ha!" Charlie replied. "Quite the improvement over elephants and peanuts, yeah Ersch?!"

Samm and Alicia both shot confused gazes at each other and then asked in unison, "Elephants and peanuts?!?"

Trying to stifle my embarrassment, I replied, "Ignore Charlie. I'm an idiot. You both were amazing. Thank you very much for inviting us."

Samm smiled and said, "Well we have a strike party to get to, and you two better get going if you want to beat the traffic. We'll catch up with you guys tomorrow."

We embraced the two of them and headed on our way.

Right before we parted, Alicia grabbed my wrist and pulled me in close like she was about to share a secret. She said, "I'm glad you didn't let your employer dictate all your waking hours." She kissed me lightly on the cheek. "Now go, before Charlie makes you walk home."

The ride home was one of those nights that you could file under the category "Endless Summer." The shadows of the buildings stretched long across the busy streets as dappled light from the setting sun flickered into my peripheral vision. We rode along with the windows down and our spirits up. I hung one arm out over the door, and Charlie was busy on his phone trying to downplay how fantastic the show was to his mother, who was clearly upset that he had taken me instead of her. I sat back, deep in thought, marveling at Samm and Alicia's performance.

I couldn't get that look in Samm's eyes out of my head. It was complete peace, utter contentment. I had never seen someone look like that before. The two of them were completely paired in the right purpose for their lives. Name it whatever you like—a calling, a passion, a vocation, a mission. It was all those things and none of them. Somehow it was more. My amazement was then interrupted by a small pang of jealousy. I had never felt that kind of peace.

My whole perspective on making a living was just a means to an end. I wasn't sure what my passions were; I'd spent so much time trying to avoid opening up to other people for fear of ridicule that I felt a little angry that there was nothing I could point to that truly stirred my heart. Charlie had his podcast, and Alicia and Samm were clearly born to perform. It occurred to me that I didn't really know what I loved to do. So much of my life was spent in financial struggle and conflict avoidance that the dreams of my heart seemed undefinable. It bothered me.

Arriving back at our apartment, Charlie tossed his phone on the counter and kicked off his shoes. His brow furrowed as he looked at me still in his clothing.

"Oh God, you better go wash my shirt—you sweat like a pig."

He headed for the door to his bedroom but stopped short, almost like he was surprised by something. He turned and said, "They were really great tonight, weren't they?"

"Yeah," I said, nodding my head in agreement. "They really were."

Charlie smiled. "That's what doing what you love looks like."

He let his words hang in the air for a second, filling the silence between us, then closed the door to his room and went to bed. I stood there for a while in the quiet darkness of our apartment, unsettled by his comment. My hands balled into tight fists, and my jaw clenched down hard. Anxiety clawed its way up into my stomach again, a deep, visceral frustration.

How could I not know what I was meant to do? The question struck me like a gut punch, and suddenly I was wheezing—sharp, shallow breaths hissing through clenched teeth. My vision narrowed, blurring. My fists, white-knuckled and trembling, pressed into the cold edge of our kitchen's breakfast bar. It felt like I was having a panic attack.

I forced myself to loosen my jaw and uncurl my fingers. Slowly, deliberately, I tried to breathe. But the calm didn't come. Instead, a wave of something darker crept in. It felt like grief, but heavier.

And at that moment, I knew—*something vital was missing.* I didn't know what it was or how to find it. But I could feel the hollow space it left behind. Had I made a huge mistake?

CHAPTER FOUR

At the Feet of the (Mc)Master

"The one thing you cannot prepare for is the passage of time."

The next few years seemed to vanish. Rather than deal with the sense of lack in my life, I buried myself in my work. Long hours became a routine. My client list grew so big I started referring people to junior associates. I dressed better and ate better, and Charlie and I went to fancier restaurants and swankier parties. We moved out of our apartment into a nicer one. His social media influence ballooned, and the walls of our place were dotted with awards from platforms he created content for.

By all definitions, I was "living the dream." However, despite my improved financial situation, that nagging sense of absence was always there. I did everything I could to distract myself—video games, CrossFit, trendy bars, binge-watching shows—but none of it made a difference. I even dated a few times. I met some wonderful women that were sociable and fun. Their companionship was always a salve for my insecurities, but none of those relationships ever withstood the time commitments of my job. All I could do was blunt the gnawing sensation that deep in my heart there was silence in the place where a song should be.

Charlie sensed it, of course, and tried to help by pushing me out of my comfort zone where he could. Most of the time, I declined. Refused is probably a better word for it. I would join him voluntarily on occasion, but half the time he forced me out with him because he knew that if I had my way, I would've never left our apartment.

In truth, my jealousy of Charlie just compounded over the years. He would drag me to events as his obligatory plus one, and almost instantly he'd have a dozen new friends while I, ever the wallflower, sat frozen on a chair waiting to be introduced. The man was like gravity. Everything was just attracted to him. He was so confident in himself—so sure of who he was.

Charlie Margolis was a master class in living on your own terms. He was able to let people's negative opinions pass through him like wind through the leaves of a tree. His resilience was incredibly irritating, sometimes. He was always excited to meet someone new and was unflinchingly optimistic that they would love him.

In contrast, I spent most of my days living on everyone else's terms. I was beholden to my job, and people generally exhausted me, which made it hard to build lasting relationships. This only perpetuated that feeling of emptiness that I carried.

One fall Sunday, while I was deep in my feelings, I asked him how he stayed so upbeat.

"It's a learned skill, Ersch. Most worthy things are," he replied, "If you put the remote down for a few days and did some soul searching, you could learn it too. Just do what I do when I'm in a rut."

I laughed dismissively. "When is the great Charlie Margolis ever in a rut? If ever someone's life seemed perfect—it's yours, my friend."

"Not true! I'm sad occasionally," he replied with a smirk.

"Doubtful."

I was annoyed. Sometimes Charlie's unshakable optimism made him seem like a Pollyanna, not that either of us had anything of substance to complain about. Still, I wasn't going to pass on the chance to ask, "Alright, Dr. Sunshine, what's your secret for getting out of a rut?"

He tilted his head a little, as if the answer should have been obvious. "I talk to Myles. The man has more wisdom in his pinky toe than either of us will have in ten lifetimes."

"Your stepdad?" I said, confused (and a little nervous). "I should talk to your stepdad? Like, alone?"

Charlie chuckled. "He won't bite you, bestie. He was there for my mother when Dad died. You remember how depressed she was. The woman didn't eat for almost a week!"

I sighed heavily and looked down at my shoes—a defense mechanism I had developed when I was nervous. Charlie knew all my tells.

He closed his book with a loud thump, sensing my apprehension. "Look, he's always made me feel better, and you've been a zombie lately. Go see Myles. Trust me." And he returned to reading.

❧❧❧❧

To catch you up, a few years after Charlie's father died, his mom Julia got remarried to a guy named Myles Duncan McMasters. He was Charlie's father's best friend growing up. He had a rough past from what I was told but eventually straightened his life out. Classic rags to riches story. Could've been a movie, I bet. Myles made his money in real estate. He and Julia lived on several secluded acres in North Greenwich near the Connecticut border.

Over the years, Myles had become like a second father to Charlie. They had a lot of similarities, like their passion for networking and relationships, but Myles didn't care for the flash (and often superficiality) of city life. He was a wise, cultured man of high integrity. I respected him a lot. That also made him incredibly intimidating. After working up the courage to message him, we made plans for me to head up to his place the following Saturday.

I'd be going alone, which made me very anxious, as my gregarious best buddy was tied up with podcast-related stuff. It was ironic. I wanted Myles's advice but was afraid of what he'd say. It was a memorable point of reflection. I was surrounded by people of incredible character, which was both a struggle and a privilege.

The entrance to Myles's property was completely unassuming. He had a black bargain-store mailbox with his name and house number in white stickers and a single-lane gravel road driveway that looked like something a lumberjack would use. His closest neighbor, for reference, had huge iron gates with stone pillars at the entrance to their property. He and Julia lived in a normal single-story home surrounded by tall pines and maple trees, again in stark contrast to the palatial estates and expertly landscaped lawns of their closest neighbors.

As I approached the front of their home, I noticed Charlie's mother Julia sitting on a large swinging bench on their front porch with an oversized flannel blanket wrapped around her, sipping a hot cup of tea, e-reader in hand. Not bad for a sunny fall morning. She looked up from her book and hopped off the bench to greet me.

"Well, if it isn't my favorite money-launderer," she said with a grin, pinching both of my cheeks. Julia Margolis never pulled her punches.

"Hi, Mama J, it's good to see you too."

She let out a sigh, hugging me. "I see my socialite son was too busy to come see his own mother?"

"Well, he is pretty popular," I said, trying to defend my buddy.

"And you think that's an acceptable excuse?" she said, clicking her tongue and staring at me through the bright-blue frames of her reading glasses. "I baked all day yesterday for the two of you, and he's not even here to enjoy it. The nerve of that child. Well, you're taking it home with you, understood?"

I raised my arms to my sides as she reached up and ran a hand through my hair. "And get a haircut, for crying out loud." We both laughed, and she said, "Well, if you'll excuse me, Inertia, my tea is getting cold, and I'm just about to find out whodunnit!" With a wink, she hurried back to her bench, grabbed the e-reader, and settled back in.

A firm hand rested on my shoulder. I turned to be greeted by that wholesome McMasters smile. Myles was about my height with straight brown hair, a salt-and-pepper beard, and weathered skin to match. He looked more like a cattle rancher than a real estate mogul. He shook my hand firmly with his strong calloused hands. "Glad you made it, Inertia. I trust the drive wasn't too difficult?"

"Hey, Mr. McMasters."

"Inertia, you're basically family. Myles is fine."

"Myles, yeah. Sorry. Drive was easy." I sighed heavily, trying to calm my nerves.

"Good." He handed me a rake. "Come on, let's go out back. I've got some things I need your help with."

Despite their modest home for their means, Myles and Julia owned the forest for almost five acres in every direction. I couldn't imagine what the property was worth. We walked to a large clearing that was thick with multicolored maple leaves.

"That's our task for today, Inertia. You're going to help me rake these leaves before the bad weather settles in."

"Rake? But Myles, I thought we were going to talk?"

"Well, you're a capable young man. Do you think you can talk *and* rake?" he replied.

"I guess so."

"Excellent. I'll start at this end. We'll meet in the middle."

Figures, I thought.

We began raking, and despite my frustrations, it did help me relax.

"So, what's eatin' ya, kid?"

I remember thinking, *here we go.*

"In a word, Myles, I feel *lost.*"

"Lost? How so?" he asked, leaning on his rake.

I could feel the discouragement in my voice, "I don't know how else to say it. And yeah, I know how ridiculous that sounds. My best friend is one of the most socially outgoing people alive. I've got a high-paying job, a cool apartment, and plenty of spending cash. I attend lots of events around town. I know. It's totally backwards. The average person would kill to trade places with me. But I feel like I'm not really doing anything. I just feel stuck."

"Stuck?" Myles shifted his weight on his rake and reached for a leaf bag. "Elaborate a little. What do you mean by stuck?"

"Ugh. I feel like a hamster on a wheel. It's like I'm just reliving the same year." I could feel myself getting angry about it. "Which is crazy! I can't even believe the things I'm saying!

'Privileged little finance bro from Manhattan feels bad about his upscale life?!' How pathetic!" I kicked a small pile of leaves.

My tone fell with my posture. "I just don't get it. I did everything I was supposed to. I climbed the ladder, bought the stuff, met the people, and went to the parties. And I'm still just … here. Just like last year, and the one before that. No purpose, no meaning, just … stuck."

"Well, no one's 'stuck,' as you put it. Wherever you are is always temporary; life is always changing, even if we don't notice it. Maybe you're supposed to feel this way right now. Maybe you're exactly where you need to be."

"What? That makes no sense. Why would I need to feel this way?"

"Well, I'm not sure. Perhaps there's something you need to learn from how you feel. So far, we've got 'lost' and 'stuck.' One word means you don't know where you are, and the other means you're someplace you can't get out of. Bit of a paradox, yeah?"

"Sweet. So, you're saying my life is one big paradox? Awesome, that's super helpful, Myles. Thanks," I replied angrily.

"That sarcasm you so frequently turn to won't help you, Inertia. It's just a defense mechanism. You don't need to use it around me. I'm not your enemy. I'm trying to help," Myles said warmly.

I kept re-explaining how I was feeling, and Myles asked where I thought those feelings were coming from. I tried to explain the things that had happened in the past, and he replied by asking why I was still hanging onto the past. This persisted for almost ten minutes. I'd say something, and he'd respond with a question. It was like the man was slowly peeling away layers of my patience.

Where was the sage advice that Charlie was talking about? I wasn't feeling better; in fact, I felt worse. My frustration was only building. I didn't know where the anger was coming from, but it slowly bubbled up into my chest, and suddenly I felt filled to the brim with a strange, unplaced rage. I stood there, looking down at the leaves, practically boiling over with anger. He asked me another question.

I had reached a breaking point.

"What do you want me to say, Myles!?!" I replied, shouting. "That I'm afraid every day?! That I wake up hating myself? That I feel like an imposter all the time?! Is that it? Do you want me to tell you that I go to bed every night wishing I was more like Charlie?! That I spend most days paralyzed by the fear of people's opinions?! That I feel purposeless, like there's a part of me that's missing?! Is that what you want to hear, Myles?! IS IT?!"

I threw the rake to the ground, sat down in a pile of leaves, and let my face fall into my hands. Myles took a knee next to me.

"You chose those words all on your own, kid, but now we've come to the heart of it. I kept pressing you because it seemed like your feelings were only symptoms. However, now it sounds like you've finally been honest with yourself out loud. Now we know what's really bothering you. And now that we've named it, we can take its power away."

I wiped my eyes and looked up at him. The old man's gaze was completely disarming. He was totally right. I was afraid to call out the real problem because it made me feel weak, powerless. The audacity, I thought, to have so much and feel so empty around it all. The shame was awful, but now that I had called it out, somehow it seemed conquerable.

"How do you do that!? I mean really?" I threw my hands to my sides. "You and Charlie both! It's crazy! You're like emotionally stable super humans! Can you fly? Do you have eye lasers? Most days, I struggle just to get out of bed!!"

Myles chuckled to himself. "No, kid, I can't fly. As for how I'm so levelheaded, well it's a learned skill; most worthy things are."

Where have I heard that before? I thought.

"I've made a lot of mistakes, Inertia. They're good teachers. I also read a lot, and I live by a few simple rules. The first of which is that *The Value Is Already in the Clay.* You aren't an imposter. You're a true friend to my stepson. Why do you think a guy like Charlie keeps a guy like you around? He'd never admit it, but you're one of the best things that's ever happened to Charlie Margolis."

Funny, because I had always thought the reverse.

"Your worth was never up for debate. Everyone has greatness inside them. Just like a lump of boring clay that becomes ornate, priceless pottery, we also need to be shaped to bring our greatness out. But it was always there. Sometimes it's just waiting for the right hour, the right event, or the right person, but the value was never in question. You just need to take some action—start shaping the clay."

It was simple yet profound. Maybe I felt this way because I was trying to run from my feelings instead of doing something about them.

"And for Pete's sake, stop comparing yourself to Charlie! You're better than that, kid. It's never fair. It's always your worst day compared to his best. You lose every time. Run your own race, against the old Inertia Hollins. Trust me, I'm just as guilty as anyone else. I compared myself to everyone I knew. It felt like everyone had it better than I did, and that drove me to do some terrible things for the approval of people I didn't even like."

I sat there for a bit, not wanting to leave my little pity party, but there was too much truth in his words. "God, Myles, you're so right. It hurts to admit it, but you're dead-on. I've been doing all the things you said I shouldn't for years now. Especially comparing myself to Charlie."

Myles nodded. "A tough act to follow, for sure. Fella like my stepson would make almost anyone insecure about themselves."

Feeling a little better, I asked him, "So, what are your other rules?"

He chuckled. "Well, the second is *Everything Is What You Make It.*"

"Huh?"

"Have you ever seen that image on the internet of the kid on the third-place podium proudly holding his medal up while the kid on the first-place podium is looking down at him with jealous eyes?" he asked.

"Yeah, I think I've seen it."

"Good. That illustrates my point very well. It doesn't matter what happens. What matters is how we respond to it. Your best day could be someone's worst; your biggest mistake could be a crossroads in your life. That's because everything seen through the lens of enough time looks a little different."

He began raking leaves again. "My father was a mean drunk. He'd get loaded and wail on me for no reason. I turned to drugs to cope, which just gave him more reason to beat me. Eventually, I ran away. Slept on my buddy Chuck's couch for months while I got clean and figured out my next move. We worked enough odd jobs and saved enough money to eventually buy a small duplex together. We rented the good side, and I remodeled the bad side while he was finishing up law school. That was my first taste of real estate, to which I owe all my financial success. By the way, Chuck, that buddy of mine? He was Charlie's dad. Imagine how different my life would be if those 'bad things' hadn't happened to me."

It was hard for me to picture a version of Myles that didn't walk on water. An abusive dad? Drug addiction? I had worked the man up in my mind to be this demigod, and from his stories, it sounded like he'd faced just as much adversity as anyone else.

A smile crept across my face. "So, everything is what you make it."

He nodded. "Now you're getting it. We might label something as bad, but it might lead to something good. Most folks don't realize that. Something doesn't have to be a big deal unless we make it one. Heck, Julia and I are living proof of that. My hand to God, I loved that woman the day I laid eyes on her. But Chuck saw her first. When they got married and had Charlie, I figured a friendship with Julia was better than nothing. When Chuck died, Julia and I helped each other grieve. I had lost my closest friend; she had lost her husband. Nothing brings people together like shared-trauma. I held onto a lot of shame about having feelings for my late friend's widow. But we've built a beautiful life together, and I think Chuck would be happy about that."

We continued to rake and bag leaves in silence as I let it all sink in. I really was making a big deal out of little things. I *did* compare myself to others way too much, especially Charlie. I did have low self-esteem despite all my outward "success."

When the yard was cleared, Myles looked down at his watch. "Alright, kid, time to wrap up. I've got to leave soon to meet up with a friend of mine to talk about a new investment."

"Seriously? Myles, if I had your money, I could burn mine! What the heck do you need another investment for? Don't you have enough?"

"Nah. Inertia, that's where folks get it wrong. I think everyone could stand to dream a little bigger. That's my third and final rule, something I like to call *Grateful Dissatisfaction*. The concept is simple—be appreciative of everything in your life, but always have something you're working toward."

I looked at him curiously.

"Let me explain. If you believe in a higher power, I don't think it designed us to live small or be average. I think we're supposed to do as much good in the world as we can, and money is a great tool for that. The trouble is, society does the opposite. We glorify people that spend their wealth conspicuously. Trust me, I went down that road before, and flashy does not equal freedom."

"Myles McMasters used to flaunt his cash?" I asked, surprised.

He nodded. "Almost bankrupted me. It was stupid. I spent so much time and money trying to impress people that I didn't know with things that I couldn't afford. Inertia, I firmly believe that for every lavish lifestyle you see on social media, there are at least a dozen quiet millionaires doing real genuine good in the world, but they never brag about it, so it mostly goes unseen."

He tossed the rakes in the back of his truck. "I believe these people surround us constantly. They don't drive a Maserati. They drive a paid-for Camry with over a hundred thousand miles on it; they live in modest homes and buy their clothes from regular stores, and their phones are always a few years old. Their possessions are tools, not statements."

He had a point. Some of my clients were like that. They didn't have a mansion or a driver, they dressed very plainly, and some of them were worth nine figures.

"Alright, Myles, I'm intrigued. So, how do these people flex on the world if they aren't conspicuous with their money?"

He smiled. "I'm sure you've seen it before. When someone's cancer GoFundMe is posted, they're the anonymous matching donation for whatever is raised. When the school needs a new roof, they quietly cover the cost. Their names cover the plaques in every hospital, school, and national park in the nation. They make the real difference in the world. They tackle the *really big* stuff but live in complete camouflage.

"And that, Inertia, is why I keep looking for my next investment. I want to be one of those people. Grateful Dissatisfaction. That's my last piece of advice to you kid—be happy with what you have while in pursuit of whatever is next."

He patted me on the shoulder. "Safe travels home. Tell my stepson to tag along next time."

❧❧❧❧

I drove home in silence with a pile of home-baked goods from Mama J and a head full of wisdom from Myles. It started to rain before I got back to our apartment. The blurry shine of the streetlights through the rainy windshield made the city come alive through the metronome of my windshield wipers.

Maybe it was time to consider another direction for my life. Maybe it was time to get off the hamster wheel and figure out what I loved to do or how I could make a bigger impact. If I died tomorrow, what difference would I have made? Who but friends and family would care, heck, or even notice? The office would replace me immediately. My clients would feign concern, but really, they'd only be concerned about their portfolios. Maybe it was time to travel more. Aside from a few short trips upstate, I'd never really left the city.

I returned to an empty apartment and a note from Charlie as I walked in.

> *Mom already texted me. Yes, I'll go with you next time. So needy. The woman is oppressive. Also, save me some baked goods, or you're dead to me. Out with Ally and Samm. The rest of my pad thai from that new place on 85th is in the fridge. The portion sizes are absurd. I ordered for myself, not the building. Anyway, help yourself and enjoy the quiet. — CM3.*

I reheated Charlie's leftovers and sat down in my favorite chair by the window. I reached for the remotes but then stopped. Hesitating, I remembered my conversation with Myles. "… *run your own race, against the old Inertia Hollins.*" So, instead, I turned to face the rainy cityscape and enjoyed my noodles.

Flipping over Charlie's note, I wrote down Myles's rules.

> *Wisdom from the (Mc)Master*
> - *The value is already in the clay: We just need to shape it.*
> - *Everything is what you make it: We can't choose what happens, only how we react.*
> - *Grateful Dissatisfaction: Be happy with what you have while in pursuit of whatever is next.*

Rereading his rules, my insides churned with a rush of newly found confidence and gurgling frustration at all the time I had wasted playing life so small. My comfort zone really had become a cage, and it was time to do something about that. It was time to make some changes—in my habits, my choices, my attitude, everything.

However, I learned quickly that when you make a big decision, life tends to test the strength of your resolve.

It was a lesson I was woefully unprepared for.

CHAPTER FIVE

Speak Easy

There are days in our lives that will remain intact in our memory forever. They are turning points, core memories, and every sound, every image, every little detail is burned in our minds.

My 29th birthday was one of those days.

Being born in late May, my birthday frequently corresponded with one of the sunset alignments of the "Manhattanhenge." If you're unfamiliar, about three or four times a year, the sun either rises or sets in perfect alignment with the skyscrapers downtown. Usually, you can catch it on 34th or 42nd Street right after the evening rush. The buildings create this "urban canyon," and the sun falls perfectly between them, setting on the horizon about a dozen blocks down the road. The brilliance of that fiery orb is on full display, coating everything in a deep reddish-orange light. I loved to stand and absorb the warmth of the sun as it slid below the horizon.

As you'd expect, this event draws the attention of every amateur photographer, social media influencer, and basically anyone with a selfie stick and a smartphone in a five-mile radius. Charlie made a point to go every year. Not to take any pictures, mind you; he couldn't be bothered with that. No, Charlie went for the crowd. Ever the networker, that guy.

This year's trip to see "the Henge" was a little more special than usual, as it happened to fall on a Friday *and* my birthday, so we were kicking off a weekend of celebration with a quick stop to see it all unfold. Charlie, in his typical fashion, kept the events of our evening a secret, telling me only to dress sharp. I obliged, not asking any questions. As I watched the final shreds of daylight vanish from sight, I looked over to see Charlie taking selfies with a few of his fans.

Eventually, my curiosity got the best of me. "So, where exactly are we going, Charlie? Why did I need to dress up to watch the Henge?"

"Don't you worry your little heart, Inertia," he said, patting me on the shoulder patronizingly. "It's going to be a fabulous evening."

He pointed ahead as two familiar faces approached. Alicia and Samm were walking toward us on 42nd Street totally dressed to kill. I was awestruck. They looked like Greek Goddesses. We're talking red-carpet, spared-no-expense, stop-traffic gorgeous.

It was a rare occasion that they both got dressed up for *anything*. Alicia usually dressed classy, but Samm was another story. She would always choose something comfortable first. I watched Samm fuss with her dress multiple times. She squirmed like a toddler forced to wear a jacket over their Halloween costume. It was obvious she was trying to be a supportive spouse but was clearly very uncomfortable. Alicia, on the other hand, looked positively giddy that she'd convinced Samm to even wear a dress.

"Wow! Ladies! I mean … Wow! You really put in maximum effort tonight! Samm, you look stunning! Is this going to be a regular thing for you now?"

She grumbled in disgust. "Easy there, science class, don't go getting any wild ideas. You and I both know as soon as I get home it's pj's and a hoodie. I'm only doing this because it's your birthday, and Charlie said we were going someplace swanky.

Speaking of swanky, look at you! Are these your clothes, or did you borrow them from Charlie again?"

"Hey, that was years ago, Kendricks. I've got my own wardrobe now."

We frowned at each other, and then a goofy smile crept across her face. I cracked my own smirk, and we both let out a laugh. Samm and I were rarely ever serious with each other. The four of us wrapped our arms around one another in our little huddle. It was a custom that Samm had started the night we all met, and it had become our regular greeting.

I turned to Charlie. "Alright, Mr. Metropcicle, you gotta give me something. What's next?"

Charlie gestured to a large black SUV parked close by with a rideshare light illuminated in the front dash. "Friends, lovers, and dreamers—our chariot awaits!" Not wanting to waste the moment, he pushed his elbows out to his sides, and Alicia and Samm both took an arm and smiled.

"Let's go, Inertia," Alicia said. "Mustn't be late for your own party."

Our ride dropped us off in Lenox Hill about five blocks from The Park at this small but exclusive-looking steakhouse with long, bright tables and a curved oak bar. The walls were decorated with these illuminated red tiles that almost looked like lava lamps and that gave the whole place this warm glow. Charlie had reserved the private meeting space in the back. There was a long table lit by ornate chandeliers above with seating for about a dozen. A few people had already arrived. Julia and Myles were there, as were my parents, Louis, and friends from work.

I hugged my folks, who I hadn't seen in a few months, quickly catching up with them before we sat down for what ended up being one of the best meals I can remember. Several courses, unique ingredients and flavors, different wine pairings with each dish—it was very special. Charlie pulled out all the stops when it came to hosting a party.

As the night carried on and guests began to say their goodbyes, Charlie spoke up. "Before you all scatter, I've got a little gift for my dear friend." He reached under the table and produced an elaborately wrapped gift bag. He handed it over to me with a warm smile.

"Many happy returns of the day, Inertia Hollins."

I gave him a big bear hug and thanked him, not having expected any gifts this year. After working my way through the copious amount of glittered ribbon and layered tissue paper, I reached in and pulled out a really nice leather-bound journal with the word "HI" branded on the cover in fancy calligraphy. Charlie had one just like it. He kept it near his reading nook and loved to keep track of his adventures in it.

"Wow, thanks for the journal, Charlie," I said appreciatively.

"You're welcome, Ersch. Now you have a place to record your own adventures," he replied.

"What's with 'HI' on the cover?" I asked.

Charlie smacked his face into his palms, "Oy Vey!"

He looked over at Alicia and Samm, who were both trying desperately to stifle a laugh. "He's not joking, is he!? Good Lord and little goldfish, Inertia Hollins, it's a miracle you survived to even see your birthday! It's upside down, genius! Those are your initials!"

Perplexed, I turned the journal over in my hand. "Oh, I guess so!" We all broke into a long laugh while Charlie just sat there shaking his head. I opened the front cover and felt the pages. It was thick mill paper, like something an ancient tome of knowledge would be written on. It felt weighty and significant in my hand. On the top left-hand side of the cover was a small note.

Find yourself. You're the only one who can. — Best, CM3

I got a little emotional. He always seemed to have precisely the right words at the right time. It was the hallmark of our relationship. I did feel lost for a long while, and I think he knew I was still trying to figure things out.

We said our farewells to our friends and family. At some point, Julia had snuck to the servers' counter, and she and Myles had covered the tab for our entire meal before any of us even had a chance to reach for our wallets. They had departed before we found out, so there was no arguing with them over who was paying. They loved doing stuff like that, especially when Charlie specifically told his mother not to.

"The nerve of that woman!" Charlie said, shaking his head, "I told her not to go all 'magnanimous benefactor' on me tonight. Every time! Could she maybe just listen to me once?! Maybe once!?"

I had to laugh. It was nice to see something get under Charlie's skin; it made him seem more human. He texted her furiously, staring down at his phone as she typed her reply. Alicia peered over his shoulder, and when Julia's response came back, she howled with laughter.

"What'd she say?" I asked.

Charlie pointed at Alicia angrily. "Not a word!"

I asked again, and he just shook his head and put his phone away. Perhaps even my level-headed best friend had his soft targets.

I turned to Alicia and Samm to thank them for a wonderful birthday celebration. Alicia smiled mischievously, saying, "Oh, darling, we're only getting started."

Samm shot Charlie a knowing smile.

"Can I tell him?"

Charlie only grinned.

"Please can I tell him?!"

"Girl, give him a hint, but you better not spoil anything," he replied.

Samm was beside herself with excitement, "OK, so, from here, we're going to someplace suuuuper special; it's the only reason I'm in this stupid dress. I can't wait for you to see it!"

We found our ride and headed off to our next location. If the city was a concrete jungle, then construction and renovation were its perennial flowers. There was always something being torn down or built up or restored. You just got used to blocked roads, detours, and walking under scaffolding almost everywhere you went. The trip to our next stop was no exception. After a few meandering road closures, we stopped in front of another restaurant. The exterior was shrouded in scaffolding and platforms. The façade was getting a much-needed update. I gave my friends a curious glance. Surely there wasn't more food planned?

"We're eating again?" I asked, a little confused.

"Not exactly," said Charlie as he produced a dark, narrow-brimmed fedora from his bag and placed it on his head. "We're here for *dessert*."

The place was loud with conversation and the sounds of dishes and food preparation. It had tall ceilings, white walls, and interesting art along the entrance way. The dining room was completely packed, and customers were already filling up any of the available waiting area. Charlie approached the servers' table, and a young gentleman in a black blazer and bow tie looked up at him.

"Do you have a reservation, sir?" he asked, looking at Charlie, to which Charlie replied, "Oh no, *friend*, we're here for the band." The server smiled, nodded, and pointed us to the back of the restaurant. "Right this way, *friends*."

It felt like there was some unspoken understanding between Charlie and the server. It was in the way that the two of them referred to each other as "friend." Something was going on.

I looked at Samm, perplexed. "There's no band here?"

To which she raised her eyebrows and shrugged. "Guess you're going to have to wait and find out, aren't cha, Ersch! Did you see my outfit?"

"It's hard to miss," I replied.

"Well, do you think I would be forced into wearing this torture chamber if it wasn't going to be worth it?"

"Good point."

We walked through the restaurant, past the myriad dinner conversations going on, past the bar full of professionals kicking off their weekends, and stopped at a small door that looked like the entrance to the kitchen. The host turned and smiled again, saying, "Enjoy your evening, *friends*."

Charlie wasted no time swinging the door open. The smell of spirits and sandalwood wafted out of the door, revealing a stairway that led down to the basement.

"OK, what is going on?!" I said nervously.

"Indulge us for a few more minutes, Inertia, and all will be revealed," Alicia said as she grabbed Samm's hand, helping her down the stairs. The stairway was dark and much longer than I expected, with a thick walnut handrail and photos on the walls of people dressed up in clothing that looked like something out of a mobster movie. I could hear music; it sounded like a jazz band or something similar. I reached the bottom of the stairs and turned the corner.

It was like stepping out of a time machine back into the roaring twenties. People everywhere were impeccably dressed but in period-appropriate attire that created an atmosphere like we really had traveled back in time. Red-leather half-circle high-back booths were crowded with revelers sharing drinks and stories by dim tea lights on the tables. There were nooks carved into the walls for more exclusive conversations and high-top tables scattered about the broad, expansive basement.

The ceiling was covered with pressed tin tiles adorned with elaborate filigree. A small, dim spotlight lit the corner where a woman in bright-red dress sang a soft melody and a square-chinned man with a stand-up bass strummed away. They were joined by a small brass section of players that picked up the pace of the music as a man behind a baby grand piano tapped out a lively tune.

"Is this"—I hesitated, lowering my voice— "a *speakeasy*?!"

Unable to contain his excitement anymore, Charlie threw his arm over my shoulder and said, "Correct you are, Inertia! This is one of the most exclusive clubs in the city. I had to pull a lot of strings to even get us on the list."

Charlie ran off to buy a round, and Alicia and Samm escorted me to a reserved booth close to the band. Everywhere, people were laughing and talking, clinking glasses, and tipping their hats to one another in an unspoken show of respect and revelry.

"Isn't this place the coolest?!" Samm said, biting her lower lip. "When Charlie told us about this place, I couldn't wait to check it out."

I had to agree. The bar was underlit with a pale-blue light that made everyone standing at it seem mysterious and alluring. The music was period perfect, right down to the lounge singer and her crew. Even the bartender was dressed in a vest with suspenders and a tight-brimmed bowler hat.

The music continued to quicken and grow louder as the dance floor began to fill up with people swing dancing. Everywhere, there was a flurry of turns, quick feet, smiles, and laughter. The vibe in this place was intoxicating. Charlie returned with a small tray of drinks and then spun around to quickly rush off again.

"You'll never guess what just happened. Remember that fun couple we met at that thing we went to uptown a few weeks ago? Well, they're here, and I'm going to go say hello!"

I hadn't the foggiest idea who he was referring to with a description like that, but I knew better than to ask a social butterfly like Charlie to clarify himself in a place like this.

As for my other two friends, Samm only needed a few notes of music before her hips started swinging and she was pulling Alicia onto the dancefloor. Having performed together for almost a decade with their troupe, the pair cut a rug like professionals. The heels came off, and they synced up their footwork almost immediately, hopping past each other with ease and grace. They changed moves with such speed and precision that it looked like they had choreographed a dance specifically for the evening. Soon after they started dancing, a small crowd began to form around them.

That was a near-perfect snapshot in time. It was raw and pure and wonderful. I could see Charlie talking and laughing with two people at the bar that looked vaguely familiar. Alicia and Samm were dancing their hearts out as the brass instruments and piano roared behind them.

The night carried on in this way till well into the small hours. Charlie introduced me to new friends and fellow influencers, and we toasted to my successful "trip around the sun." At one point Charlie and Alicia danced a little quickstep while Samm was getting water, and Samm even succeeded in pulling me out onto the dance floor for a few songs. It was a banner night on all counts.

By the time we surfaced again, the restaurant above us was dark and quiet, with only a few people still at the bar. The skies had clouded over, and steady rain dappled against the windows, filling our vision with droplets of reflected light from the streets. We were all thoroughly exhausted but riding high on the events of the evening. Navigating the damp, narrow, scaffolded walkways, we headed for the end of the block.

And then, like in any defining moment in life, everything changed in an instant.

Our rideshare driver was parked across a busy street, and we needed to cross quickly to get to him. Construction blocked one of the roads, so he was as close as he could get. I had the idea to just cut through the cars and get there fast to get out of the rain quicker. There was a green moving truck stopped at a stoplight, and I saw the headlights of a garbage truck far enough away that I thought we could make it. The rain intensified as I stepped into the street. Alicia and Samm followed behind Charlie when I heard him yell. The driver of the garbage truck was distracted, texting. He didn't see the moving truck stopped in front of him. Charlie shoved Alicia and Samm back over the curb, leaving the two of us in the gap.

I realized what was happening too late.

I couldn't think. I couldn't react. It happened in an instant, but then again it seemed like everything was in slow motion. Charlie shoulder-checked me clear of the garbage truck but into traffic. Almost immediately, my legs were knocked out from under me as I was hit by an oncoming car. The side of my head struck the windshield of the car hard enough that I heard a loud crack. I wasn't sure if it was my head or the glass that made the sound. The last thing I remember, before rolling off the vehicle and falling onto the street, was watching Charlie close his eyes and then disappear between the vehicles as they collided.

CHAPTER SIX

Used to the Darkness

"CHARLIE!" I screamed as I staggered over to him.

The vehicles had separated, and Charlie had collapsed on the street. I don't remember much other than screams and yelling, people calling for emergency services. The spot where my head had impacted the car's windshield began to bleed, and the rain mixed with blood as it dripped from the side of my head. I could barely see through the tears and the rain.

I kept repeating his name over and over as I fell to my knees next to him, grabbing his hand and propping his head up in my arms. He squeezed my hand back tightly and opened his eyes. He looked up at me with anguish. I couldn't begin to imagine the pain he was in. He strained to speak, and I just kept shouting his name. His grip tightened even further. Eyes and body trembling, soaked in rain and blood, he managed through haggard breathing to say five simple words.

"Don't … be sad for me."

Then his face relaxed into a soft grin.

His grip eased up, and his trembling stopped.

His eyes gently closed with a long exhale, and Charles Margolis the Third, the single greatest human that had entered my life to that point, died in my arms.

❦ ❦ ❦

It seemed impossible. Every hour, every minute, I expected him to call, to text, or to just walk through the door. I was convinced that I had dreamed a vivid nightmare and that my best friend was still alive. It was inconceivable that someone so loved and so cherished by so many would have been taken from us, taken from me, in his prime. Fate could not be so hopelessly cruel. Yet the deafening silence of the apartment told a different story. There I was, amid all his things. His pictures and awards lined the walls. His clothing was still strewn over one end of the couch. His personal effects surrounded me, but I was alone. Truly alone.

The days immediately following Charlie's death were a blur. I was overwhelmed everywhere I looked. Replaying the events leading up to that fateful moment, I scrutinized every detail— blaming the weather, the garbage truck, the construction, the city, but mostly myself. I couldn't stem the pain. It was like hanging onto a live electrical wire. It was too much; all I could do was yell and cry until my eyes ran dry.

I stopped answering my phone despite the near nonstop calls and texts. It was too hard to keep re-explaining the accident to the next person, so I shut everyone out. My boss Louis was very understanding. When I called to tell him the news and ask for time off, contrary to the typical suck-it-up sentiment of the finance world, his response was surprisingly compassionate.

"Hollins, with the clients you've brought in? Take all the time you need, kid. I'll manage your accounts myself if necessary."

"Thanks, Louis, that means a lot."

It was a simple mercy that let me grieve in the only way I knew how. Silence. Disbelief. Anger. I drew all the curtains in the apartment and just remained there. Those were the longest days of my life. I didn't even bother to turn on any lights after dusk. I just curled up on my couch, frozen from grief in the darkness.

About five days after the accident, my silence became a problem. A few texts came through from Samm, full of concern and frustration at my lack of communication. I ignored them.

The bright-blue light of my phone lit up the space around me as another text came in. I looked down at it. Samm again, this time in all caps. They were on their way over. About an hour later, the buzzer above my mailbox sounded, and the voice of a very nervous Samm Kendricks filled the apartment. I could tell by the slight tremble in her tone that she had been crying.

"Inertia, we're here. You better open this door right now, or I'm calling 911, and emergency services will break it down for me!"

I mustered the courage to buzz them in because I could tell from the frustration in Samm's voice that the 911 threat was not a bluff. A few minutes later, there was a loud banging on the door. I opened it, and there was Samm, black eyeliner streaming down the sides of her cheeks. She wiped her face quickly and sniffled. Her typical bubbly smile was replaced with an angry scowl. She jumped forward and shoved me with both hands, knocking me back against the breakfast bar as she stormed through the door.

"Answer your stupid phone, you big jerk! We were worried sick about you!"

She immediately threw her arms around me in an enormous hug as she began to sob on my shoulder. She squeezed me so hard I thought she might break my ribs.

"I'm sorry, Samm. I didn't mean to worry you," I said between short gasps for air.

"Shut up and hug me back, dummy! And don't ever do that again!" she said through muffled tears as she rubbed her face into my hoodie. I drew my arms up around her shoulders and squeezed her back. Fresh tears began to fall down my own cheeks.

Alicia stepped through the door with grocery bags in her hands. She rubbed Samm's shoulder for a second, wiped her own eyes, then grabbed my chin, inspecting the bandage on the cut above my temple from when I collided with the car windshield.

"When's the last time you ate anything?" she asked sternly.

I shrugged, not able to remember when my last meal was.

"That's what I thought. I'm cooking. You're eating," she said with a stiff nod.

"Ally, I'm really not that hungry."

She raised an eyebrow and glared at me for a second. "I'm sorry, did you misunderstand that as a choice? You're eating, Inertia."

Not having the emotional reserves to argue, I shrugged, agreeing. Samm released her stranglehold on me and lifted her head. "Sorry for pushing you," she said remorsefully.

"It's OK, Samm," I replied.

I walked over to the couch and plopped down, letting my head drop back against the cushions. She followed me, crawled into a tight ball in my lap, dug her face back into my hoodie, and began to cry again.

"No! It's not OK, Inertia! Nothing's OK! I don't know how to fix this! I can't bring Charlie back! I can't make you feel better, and I can't stop crying. I don't know how else to help, so I'm just going to stay here and take up space in your lap until Ally finishes dinner."

That was enough. We just sat there together, swallowed up by our sorrow, and kept space for each other. It helped. Sometimes we don't need a solution. Sometimes we just need some company.

The smells of sizzling food slowly filled the apartment. Alicia was not a classically trained chef, but she knew her way around a kitchen better than most. I didn't realize how hungry I was until the smell of her cooking filled the room. She busied herself with chopping veggies and stirring a saucepan as she added ingredients and periodically wiped her eyes.

Alicia was old school. She tended to show affection through deeds and frustration through silence. She rarely let her raw emotions show, and when she did, you knew it was serious. Amid her ingredient chopping, she stopped for a minute and approached us on the couch, chef knife in hand, face full of anger. Wiping tears from her eyes again and pointing the knife directly at my face, Alicia boiled over like a kettle.

"You've got a lot of nerve, Inertia Hollins, shutting us out like that! Do you have any idea how many people have been trying to get ahold of you?! Did you know that your own parents had to call me to figure out what happened?! Who do you think has been handling things with Julia and Myles while you sulk in the dark?! I know you're grieving, but that's no excuse to push us away! We're grieving too! He saved all of us, Inertia! Not just you! We *all* might have been crushed by that truck had it not been for Charlie."

I shrugged, defeated. "I'm sorry, Ally. I'm sorry for everything," I said, shaking my head.

This is rock bottom; it must be, I thought.

She paused for a minute, noticing that the knife was still in her hand and still pointed at my face. She shook her head quickly and lowered her arm, regaining her composure. "I'm sorry too," she said softly. "You didn't deserve that."

Samm's muffled voice called out from under my arms, "Yes, he did!"

There was silence for a second, and then the three of us burst into a mixture of laughter and tears. Alicia set the knife down and helped me and Samm off the couch.

We sat down to eat. It was a quiet meal, uncharacteristic of our crew, but we were a seat shy, and the existence of that vacancy weighed heavy on all our hearts.

⊰⊱⊰⊱

The driver of the garbage truck that caused the accident was eventually brought up on charges of negligent homicide. I didn't care. Any need for justice was gone at that point. Even mentioning the details felt like re-opening the wound. Legal recourse wasn't going to bring him back.

Between fits of sobbing and rage and throwing things around my apartment, I was overcome with this pervasive suffocating apathy. It laid over me like a heavy blanket or a thick fog and slowed everything in my life to a crawl.

Samm and Alicia visited every Wednesday and Sunday night. Alicia would cook; Samm would sit with me. It helped to have them around because when I was alone with my thoughts, I was basically a zombie. I struggled through each day, and my sleep was plagued with nightmares. Every morning, I was confronted with the cold reality again. He was gone. I had lost my lighthouse, and I was hopelessly adrift at sea.

Services for Charlie were held near Julia and Myles's home two weeks after the accident. It was an amazing sight. Hundreds and hundreds of people showed up for the calling hours. Julia stood in the receiving line, flanked by me and Myles. She held both our hands tightly as each person paid their respects. As sad as I was about losing my best friend, my heart broke for her. No parent should ever have to bury their child.

The funeral home was packed solid. Fans of *Metropcicle* arrived by the dozen. Tons of our old buddies from high school and college came too. Family, friends, even other content creators and media managers from affiliated channels flew into the services. It felt like the whole world had come to say farewell to my best friend.

Thinking back on it now, what a privilege it was to be so close to such a rare soul. I counted fifty-seven separate flower arrangements in the funeral home.

Julia was crippled with grief and asked that I speak at the calling hours for her. Hundreds of sad faces filled the crowded room as I approached a small podium next to a picture of my best friend. The deep ache in everyone's hearts was palpable. A weighty sadness hung in the air. I thanked them all for coming and shared the particulars about the reception after the services.

As for what to say about Charlie, I was at a loss for words. How could I sum up a life such as his with a eulogy? How could I describe his value? There was nothing that I could say that would do him justice, so I decided to keep it very short. I looked out into the teary eyes of everyone gathered and said plainly, "He was the best of us."

⬧⬧⬧⬧

Alicia and Samm had offered to host the reception at their apartment. The steady hum of conversation filled the air as guests from the calling hours filled their place. Despite the distance and the traffic, many of those that had come to pay their respects also followed us back into the city to continue the celebration of our dear friend. I tried my best to mingle, but not only was it painful, it was still a challenge for me to be outgoing and personable. Typically, I relied on Charlie for that.

After some time, I departed the growing crowd of well-wishers and made my way up to the patio. My head was still a little sore from the collision with the car on the night of the accident. I rubbed the area as I walked by Alicia. She gently squeezed my hand. She was talking with some fellow performers from their troupe. She watched me walk past as I hopped up on the ledge of the building and let my legs dangle over the side. I sat there for some time, questioning if I would ever feel joy again. There was a roiling agony in the pit of my chest. I sat on the ledge, staring down at the street below, wondering if it would be easier to just leap off and rejoin my friend.

Survivors guilt, I've heard it called.

It's a strange condition. It follows you everywhere like a shadow and holds your hand like a sad, lost child, except you're the one that feels sad and lost. It can be summed up in a simple sentence, "It should have been me."

Illogical, I know. Ridiculous, I know. It sounds crazy. It *is* crazy.

However, unless you are one of the rare individuals that has experienced tragic loss directly, but by some miracle you survived, then this private pain will be hard to understand. It's a pervasive feeling of wanting to end your life if it meant another might live.

"It should have been me."

The words fell bitterly from my mouth as I spoke them into the air. I knew in my heart I couldn't bring him back, but at that time I would have traded anything to see him again, even my own life.

In my grief, I didn't notice Alicia approach. Instead of a comforting hand on my shoulder, she grabbed the back of my belt tightly and yanked it toward her.

"Stop it!" she said angrily.

"Stop what?" I replied, confused.

"You know exactly what, Inertia Hollins!"

I turned to face her as she pointed her finger at me with her free hand. "You think we all aren't in pain, that we all aren't just as sad as you are?! You think that's the way out?! That this is what Charlie would want?! Stop being so blindly selfish! I miss him too—desperately— every day. But I refuse to compound that grief by suffering the loss of someone else I love! Now get off this ledge or, Goddess help me, I will drag you off it in front of all our guests!"

I hopped down off the ledge. In the fog of my grief, I wasn't entirely focused on what she said, but one word stood out to me.

"Love?"

SMACK

Alicia slapped me, hard, and right across the face, her eyes full of fury.

"Oh, blessed be, Inertia, are you really that thick? Yes! Of course I love you, you stubborn, foolish man! So do Samm and Mrs. Margolis, and Myles, and practically everyone here! Now pull yourself together!"

"I'm sorry, Ally. I just ... It just hurts, constantly. I keep asking myself the same question: Why him?"

Her rage quickly melted into compassion as she rubbed her fingers over the bright red handprint that was now forming on my face. "I know. I feel the same way. There's really no explanation for this life, I'm afraid. At least none that will help your heartache. Sometimes I feel like it's just random awful days like this one scattered amongst all the rest. But sadness subsides with time and company. My mother said that to me once. Listen, I'll continue to be strong for you, but I need you to reciprocate. Can you do that?"

I managed a soft smile and a nod.

"Good." She grabbed both sides of my face, rose up on her toes, and kissed my forehead. "Come sit with us, Inertia. If there's one thing you don't need, it's more isolation."

Alicia was a rare soul. She had the tenderness and wisdom of a grandmother with the proper manners of a Victorian lady. It was almost as if she was born during the wrong century. She was quick to forgive and deeply giving and sincere. She was one of those people that you never wanted to disappoint but that always had your back after you ultimately did. Everyone needs an Alicia D'Archangelis in their life.

The day concluded with Myles, Julia, Samm, Alicia, and me sitting around their living room, laughing and crying about the late, great Charles Margolis the Third. Julia kept hugging us all through bouts of tears.

"There's this line from a movie that Charlie loved," Julia said, sniffling, as she grabbed a tissue. "I don't remember it completely; it was some sci-fi movie—you know I don't watch that stuff. Now, I'm paraphrasing, but it was something like, '*The biggest flames don't burn nearly as long, and you have burned very so brightly* ...' That was my son. He burned so very brightly."

Myles and Julia headed home for the night, and I stayed after to help with the cleanup. Samm, already dressed down in flannel pants and a tank top, punched me in the arm gently. "See you for dinner tomorrow, science class. We'll be there at six."

"Travel safe, Inertia. It's late," Alicia added.

We encircled one another with our arms, resting our foreheads against each other's in our signature friend huddle. It was comforting but also hard.

The circle was a little smaller now.

I stepped out onto the street, and the clouds, almost as if on cue, opened into a downpour. The tears still streaming down my face completely vanished in the rain. Typically, I would have raced to the garage where my car was parked, but the rain felt intensely purifying. So, I walked at an even pace and let it wash over me.

Under all my sorrow over losing my best friend, the desperate longing that I had left unnamed sat quietly, waiting for me to notice it again. On my way home, it resurfaced, only now, instead of something left unfinished, it felt like an enemy. It was as if it was rising up against me like a dragon or a demon that I had to slay. I gripped the steering wheel tightly. Letting out a loud yell in anger, I punched the dashboard. There was no Charlie Margolis to lean on anymore. I could not rely on his charm and charisma to guide me through the dark forest that grew in my mind. My search for greater purpose was no longer just important, it was necessary.

CHAPTER SEVEN

Fireside Discoveries

It was an average Thursday in late August, about three months since the accident. I wasn't sleeping well. A couple of times a week, I'd have terrible nightmares and wake up in a cold sweat, screaming Charlie's name. It left me feeling unsettled all the time.

However, that rainy evening on the way home from his services made me hyper-focused on discovering my purpose and passions. Time seemed very precious, and I was no longer willing to be a spectator in my own life. Something had to change, but I still didn't have any idea what that was. I returned to work and attacked my responsibilities like a starving animal, channeling my frustration into the job. Whatever came next, I'd need money to live off—so I cut out almost all unnecessary spending and saved almost half of my pay.

Stepping into the apartment after an uneventful commute home, I scanned my surroundings. Pictures, letters, flowers, fan art, and other memorabilia from Charlie's followers still crowded the countertops. His media manager dropped them off periodically, and I couldn't bring myself to get rid of any of it.

I admired everything with a somber smile like I did most days and headed for the fridge. I decided to keep the apartment, *our apartment*, at least until the lease ran out. Just then, my phone rang. It was Julia FaceTiming me. She never texted anymore— something about needing to connect better.

"Hey, Mama J, what's up?"

Julia's warm smile and soft voice came over the phone. "Inertia, hello dear." There was lingering sadness in her eyes that seemed like it might never leave. She paused for a second, steadying her voice. I'm sure the sight of our apartment in the background was bittersweet.

"Listen, we're headed upstate this weekend, and it would mean a lot to me if you joined us. I have something of Charlie's I need to give you. Invite the girls too."

"What's upstate?" I asked.

"Myles found a vacation rental with some serious character right on Tupper Lake in the Adirondack Park—sleeps eight. Got a nice firepit and water access. They have a craft fair this weekend, and there's some nature place Myles wants to go back to. I think getting out of the house will do me some good. Anyway, while I'm busy at the fair, the three of you can accompany Myles on his little jaunt into the wilderness or whatever. I'd prefer him to have company so he doesn't get eaten by a bear or some other nonsense. Will you join us?"

I hated leaving the city, but a few days in the woods seemed like it might give me time to think, time to sort out more of my emotions.

"Yeah, you know what, that sounds good. I'll clear my schedule. You're right, we could all probably use a little time away," I said.

A flicker of her old self returned. "I'm always right, Inertia."

I smiled. There was a short pause of reflection between the two of us, and it seemed like we could both sense the hurt in each other's eyes.

"How are you holding up?" I asked.

I could tell she wasn't ready for the question. She looked down, her chin quivering a little as she wiped her left eye.

"I have good and bad days." She looked back up at the screen. "How about you?"

My voice caught in my throat. I could feel my eyes starting to water. "About the same."

She nodded. "Pack for the weekend. Come up to the house after work tomorrow, and we'll all ride up together."

"See you then."

❦❧❦❧

I pulled up to their home the next day to see Samm loading bags and Alicia talking with Myles.

"Perfect timing," Samm said with a grin, dropping their bags in front of the car. "You can finish up."

I rolled my eyes and stepped out of the car. "Too much for you, Kendricks?"

Samm's hands balled up into fists, and she took a quick step toward me, feigning a punch. "Thanks for your help, Ersch."

I nodded, grabbing the bags.

Julia stepped out of their house and raised her hands to her sides, "Ah, wonderful. There you all are! I'm so glad you could make it." Julia made her rounds to each of us, offering up a big hug.

The drive up was comfortable, despite the three of us in the back. Alicia sat to my left. She leaned against the window, quickly falling asleep. Samm, on my right, threw her legs over my lap and did the same. After about an hour, Julia pulled out her book and began reading.

"I don't know how you can read in a car, Mama J. I'd get about a paragraph finished, and then the nausea would kick in," I said from the back seat as we rolled along the highway.

"It's a learned skill, Inertia. Most ..."

"I know, I know ... *most worthy things are,*" I said, finishing her sentence.

Myles looked up into the rearview mirror with a slight smirk on his face. Turning to Julia, he said, "You might be right, dear, he might be ready."

"Ready for what?" I asked.

Julia nodded her head slowly, patting Myles on the leg as she whispered, "I'm always right, sweetheart."

"Ready for what?" I repeated, intrigued by the exchange.

Myles met my eyes in the rearview again. "Ask us again before we head home for the weekend, Inertia. Now's not a good time."

I sat back in my seat, slightly irritated.

Tupper Lake is one of those picturesque mountain towns. Rolling hills, winding roads, and pine trees surround a deep freshwater lake with lots of little coves and nooks along its shoreline. My parents loved to camp when I was little, but it had been almost a decade since I'd seen woods like these.

We arrived at what appeared to be an elaborate contemporary log cabin with a handful of oddly shaped additions stuck onto sections of the main home. Some were suspended in the air on tall support posts; others looked partially subterranean, like in a split-level home.

"Sleeps eight?!" I said, walking through the large six-foot-wide front door. "Are you sure they didn't mean eighty?!"

The place was enormous.

The front door opened to a massive lofted great room with a center column stone fireplace and what appeared to be small stairways leading off into at least a half dozen smaller spaces. The giant A frame of the main room met at a point against an entire wall of glass that looked out over the lake. Over our heads ran a long, twisting staircase that led up to several bedrooms.

Despite its size, the space was filled with things. Almost every hard surface was covered with stacks of dusty books, trinkets, bottles of spices and herbs, candles that had dripped wax onto the hardwoods, pressed flowers, and tiny paintings. Small plants hung almost everywhere. Huge bird-of-paradise and philodendrons taller than any of us stood proudly in enormous pots at each corner. Driftwood, semi-precious stones, crystals, and stained glass surrounded us.

Pine branches made wreaths that were decorated with odd little glass ornaments. Tapestries filled one wall; a jar of writing quills stood on an end table, and everywhere we looked there were neat little stone figurines, sketches, walking sticks. It was like entering into the museum of someone's life—all the items of value that they had collected over decades condensed into one space. We were surrounded by the story of their adventures.

The place was cluttered but somehow felt comfortable. Like you could exist in this space for years and never grow bored because there was always something new to uncover or rediscover.

"I told you the place had some serious character," Julia said with a grin.

In the center of it all was a worn leather sectional couch surrounding a huge, shaggy ottoman that looked like the gathering place for any that had come to stay a while and listen to the many tales of the fantastical wizard or sorceress that must have called this menagerie their home.

"Julia Margolis does not disappoint," Alicia said with a wide smile while nodding her head and scanning the room.

We all wandered around the home for a bit, checking out all the intricate and elaborate items that lay before us. Myles busied himself with a book on woodworking that was resting on top of a stack of old books. Julia spun the little suncatchers that hung in the window frames, sending bits of colored light in fun little patterns in every direction. Samm dove onto the couch. I wandered my way up the stairs, admiring the tall fireplace flue and the elaborate stonework that encapsulated it. There was a decent-sized room which I claimed for the weekend.

Julia and Myles went out back to inspect the wide stone pathway that led to a large firepit surrounded by Adirondack chairs that overlooked a small dock. I leaned over the lofted balcony, my mind still buzzing in anticipation. Julia had something for me, something of Charlie's, something that I was "ready for" as Myles had put it. I went to bed wondering what it might be.

My dreams were full of troubled memories, like usual. It was mostly just images now, sounds and flashes of light, noises, screeching tires, yelling. I had hoped that a night away from familiar surroundings would help me sleep better.

"Maybe someday," I spoke quietly as I rolled back over in bed.

The next morning, the smell of breakfast filled my nose as I walked down the stairs to see Myles sifting through old books. Alicia and Samm were both sitting on the dock—coffee in hand, feet in the water.

"Ah, there he is," Myles said. He was seated at a high-top chair near a drafting desk at the end of the great room. He raised his mug to me, took a short sip, and said, "Julia's at the fair already, the ladies are on the dock, coffee's still hot, and there's plenty of eggs left on the counter."

"Thanks, Myles, coffee and eggs sounds awesome right now."

"How'd you sleep?" he asked, gesturing toward the coffee pot.

"Same as usual," I replied with a short sigh.

"Still having nightmares?"

I nodded. He nodded back.

"It's hard for all of us, Inertia. I'm still in a bit of disbelief myself. I'm not going to try and sell you a piece of blue sky, life isn't always kind or fair, but don't let its ugliness and unfairness overwhelm you. Nothing is constant, and this too shall pass."

I rubbed my hand through my hair as I headed for the kitchen. "Ugh, no universal wisdom before breakfast, Myles," I groaned. "I need caffeine and calories before I can handle any more profound insight."

He chuckled to himself. "Fair enough."

There was a small pamphlet on the counter near the coffee maker with a funny little circular logo on it in the shape of an otter.

"The Wild Center?" I asked. "Is this the place we're going today?" I flipped through the brochure. "It looks like the kind of place you take fifth graders for a field trip. You drove all the way up here for this?"

"Don't be too hasty. I've been vacationing in the Adirondacks most of my life. The place tends to surprise you. They have a cool boardwalk I think you'll like."

I shrugged. "Alright, Myles. I'll take your word for it."

We pulled up to a large, three-story, octagon-shaped center building with large outbuildings attached on two sides. We entered a seating area that was eye level with the pond out back. A neat little aesthetic that I took note of. Myles wandered off, while Alicia, Samm, and I walked around, checking out the exhibits. As we caught back up with Myles, he waved us over to the side exit.

"I thought you were lost," he said with a chuckle.

"It's not a big building, Myles. Did you forget where we live?"

"There's that signature sarcasm! Excellent. Come with me. Time to show you why we came here."

We followed a small path toward something called the Wild Walk.

"This looks like fun!" Samm said excitedly.

The Wild Walk is a thirty-foot-high boardwalk that takes you up over most of the treetops that surround the nature center. The Adirondack Forest unfurls in every direction for miles. We made our way up an interconnecting system of bridges and walkways to see a riot of colors expand before us. We were far enough north that the fall foliage had started to bloom again. Tall green pines stood stoic between amber birches and crimson sugar maples. Copper-toned beeches dotted the rolling hills. It was a sea of autumn but also very poignant, like most things these days.

Charlie would have loved this, I thought.

We stood there for a while, not saying anything to each other. Alicia broke the silence while staring off into the distance. "There's a saying that trees lose every leaf they have each year and yet stand tall and wait for winter to pass, and every year in spring they are rewarded. I know you feel like you've lost all your leaves, Inertia—we feel it too. But maybe this is just a period of winter for us."

"Wise words," Myles said. He looked down at his phone. "It's Julia. I'll be right back," he said as he stepped away.

"Ally makes a good point, Ersch. Heck, you aren't even thirty yet. A lot of your story isn't written, and who knows, maybe someday it'll be part of someone else's survival guide," Samm added with a nod.

I smiled. A good one. It had been a while. I looked at them and said, "You're better friends than I deserve."

It felt like an apology rather than a compliment, long overdue and scarcely adequate for how much support they had shown me. It was amazing how much I needed them all. Companionship was as vital to me as air and water. It would have been easy for me to just harden my heart and become convinced that I was strong enough or resilient enough to take life on alone—like some kind of superhero.

But I couldn't. In fact, no one can. Teams are always stronger than heroes. People need people. A truth I was slowly learning. I shook my head, looking down at the ground far below us. "I'm very lucky to have you both."

Samm let out a giggle. "We know."

The three of us stood there, eyes lost in the horizon. Maybe Alicia was right, and I was just "wintering" while waiting for better days. Maybe Samm had a point, and someone would benefit from my story someday. They were hopeful thoughts, and those were in short supply lately.

Myles walked back over to us, putting his phone back in his pocket.

"Worth the trip?" he asked.

The three of us glanced at him with grateful nods.

"Good. Julia's back from the craft fair. She said the house is, and I quote, 'too big and too weird' for her to be there all by herself. It'll be a great night for a campfire. If you're ready, we should head back."

⋐⋑⋐⋑

We arrived back at the cabin to find Julia pulling a cart of logs from the side of the house to the backyard near the firepit. She was clearly glad to see us and promptly gave the handle of the cart to Myles.

"Thank you, dear," she said through heavy breaths. "I would have finished, but since you're here, you can take over."

Samm walked out to the dock, kicked off her flip-flops, dropped her feet in the water, and lay flat on her back. I followed her out to the edge, looking out at the lake.

"Why don't you dip your toes in, Ersch? Wait, can you even swim?" she asked through squinted eyes staring up at me.

"Sure, I can swim! What kind of question is that!?" I replied.

"Well, I don't know! I've never seen you leave the city—not a lot of lakes in Manhattan."

I rolled my eyes, "Whatever, Kendricks."

"Whatever yourself, Hollins!" she said, sticking her tongue out at me.

The sun gradually set behind the tall pines that surrounded the lake, but not before turning the whole surface of the water bright orange. We made a nice fire down by the water and sat around it on the big red Adirondack chairs. Myles shared stories of some of the trouble he and Charlie's father got into when they were roommates. I shared one of the more embarrassing stories from my college years that Charlie and I swore to keep a secret.

"It was during the school renovations our sophomore year, about a month before Charlie launched his podcast. We had been out late partying with friends," I said, leaning forward in my chair. "We decided it was a good idea to go check out the construction zone. I remember it was snowing, and it was that soft, pillowy holiday-movie snow. It covered everything in a thin white blanket."

I looked around to see the four of them leaning in with me, eager for the rest of the story.

"So, we might have found the heavy equipment, and I might have had the brilliant idea to check them all for keys. Do you remember that email that went out about the varsity field damage?" I asked.

There was a moment of shock and realization on Julia's face.

"Oh my God! You mean the incident with the steamroller?!"

"That was us," I said with a grin.

"My son stole *a steamroller*?!" Julia said, flabbergasted.

"It was enormous. We drove it for a few hundred feet, and then we crushed a large section of the fence to get on the football field so we could do a few donuts near the fifty-yard line. Charlie kept the keys. I think they're still in our apartment back home," I replied.

Myles let out a roar of laughter.

"Stop it!" Julia chided, slapping him on the knee, barely able to control her own laughter. "That's not true! Not my Charlie!" She shook her head in surprise. "Inertia! Why didn't you ever say anything?! It's been almost a decade since you two were in school!"

I shrugged. "Well, the damage to the fence was significant, and Charlie thought it would be best if we let the statute of limitations run out before we said anything about it, and then we just kinda forgot."

"Oy vey!" she said, falling back into her chair. "You're in big trouble, Charles Margolis!" she added, pointing an angry finger at the sky. "Well, that boy of mine sure was full of surprises."

"Speaking of surprises," I said. "What is this thing you have of Charlie's?"

She looked over at Myles and then back at me. Then she reached down by the side of her chair and handed me a small box. I looked down at it but was suddenly afraid.

"I don't know if I want to open it," I said, uncertain.

"Why not?" she asked.

"I don't know if I want to see something of his. It might be too painful."

Julia smiled lovingly. "I understand, dear. Better than anyone. I've been struggling with those same feelings. It's different for the parent, especially the mother. I'll bear the sadness of his passing forever."

She patted Myles on the leg. "But this man has been very helpful, just like when we lost my husband. Remember what you told me dear, 'If you close your heart off to pain, you also close it off to joy.'"

That sounded like something Myles would say.

Julia glanced back over at me. "Open it."

I looked down at the box, still unsure. Removing the cover, I looked down to see something very familiar to me.

"His notebook? The one he kept in his reading nook? I've seen this thing a thousand times. Why give it to me now?"

"Because of the last few pages," she replied.

I opened it. There were doodles, drawings, and notes about restaurants, parties, and people. There were pages full of quotes from books he had read. He kept a detailed record of anything he saw, read, or heard that he deemed important. It was like thumbing through the archives of his mind. I flipped to the end and saw it, my name at the top of one of his entries. As I read the note, it felt like I could hear his voice in my head.

So ... my very best friend in the whole world, Inertia Hollins, is blue these days. Downright melancholy. It's obnoxious! The man has everything anyone with any common sense could ever hope for, including the most excellent roommate imaginable—yours truly.

Anyways, despite my quite considerable and extraordinary efforts, which he does not deserve, he continues to carry on this sad disposition. I have taken this manchild to every social engagement in the city save for the Met Gala—because, let's face it, Inertia wouldn't last an hour among that crowd. (He was right.) None of it, children, has brightened the poor boy up one bit. So annoying, this mood of his.

Thus, I am left with only one choice, to get those sad brown eyes of his out of the city and onto different places. I am henceforth beginning my glorious plot—The Inertia Hollins World Tour!

Well, maybe the world is a bit much. Maybe we'll start with our own country first. I digress. I will bring my sad, apathetic friend to so many amazing places that his heart will surely explode! Outstanding! It's settled! To Arms! We ride at dawn! Well, it's cold out. Maybe we ride after his birthday, or perhaps during the summer. Probably summer.

Cheers, darlings. – CM3."

Below his colorful monologue, there was a small list of places, far from the city. Places we hadn't really talked about in all our years of friendship. Places he wanted us to go. On each page after that there were details on the locations—spots to go see, places to eat, attractions and excursions that we could go on.

Julia interrupted my reading. "He'd been planning this for some time. He even started saving money in a separate 'adventure account' specifically for it. When he told me his plans, I protested, unsure if it was a good idea to be gone that long. And in typical Margolis fashion, he quoted an author or philosopher to prove his point. This time it was Mark Twain. He said, 'Mother! Travel is fatal to prejudice, bigotry, and narrow-mindedness, and many of our people need it sorely on these accounts. Broad, wholesome, charitable views of men and things cannot be acquired by vegetating in one little corner of the earth all one's lifetime.'"

I smiled. That was classic Charlie Margolis. The perfect line for every occasion.

"That's what he was afraid you were doing," Julia continued. "Vegetating in your little corner of the earth. There are some great places on his list and enough in the account to pay for most of it."

I was awestruck and, admittedly, afraid. I hated travel. I liked the city. As busy and crowded and expensive as it was, it was home. "I'm not sure if I can do this, Mama J. One of these places is international! I mean, the first place on the list is the other side of the continent!"

"You'll learn to look forward to the discomfort of unfamiliarity, Inertia. You need to trust me on this, dear. I've never felt more alive than when I was exploring something or someplace new," she replied.

I recoiled at the comment. It was too big a task, too painful a journey, especially alone. Also, like most people, I was very comfortable living within a ten-mile radius of my front door. I rarely, if ever, ventured outside my own personal geographical fence. Even this trip up north was a stretch for me.

I started to breathe quicker, my palms beginning to sweat. Leaning over in my chair, I tried to settle my breathing. The first location on the list was farther west than I had ever traveled in my life. The anxiety was crippling. It made me dizzy. It was like I couldn't get enough air in my lungs. However, in that moment, the same quiet longing that had dogged my thoughts for years urged me to fight the fear.

These were effectively Charlie's last wishes. The trip we never got to take. I would dishonor his memory if I didn't go. My emotions were a rollercoaster. Sorrow mixed with fear; apprehension and excitement clouded together. Frustrated resolve crawled up my shoulders like a pair of grasping hands, and just like on the ride home from his services, I was suddenly filled with grit and determination. Perhaps this was the change I had been searching for, the change I knew I needed.

"Well, how do I get to Yellowstone?" I asked, a small fire of tenacity flickering in my eyes.

Myles folded his arms, nodding in admiration. "Probably by plane, kid."

CHAPTER EIGHT

Perspective in the Park

"Live in New York—but leave before it makes you hard," I muttered, quoting the classic commencement speech as I rolled my eyes and boarded my flight out west. It had been a few weeks since that fateful evening in Tupper Lake, and my apprehension had resurfaced. This felt like a mistake. I was traveling to some tiny little town for what? To head into the woods and see some geysers? Maybe that infamous New York City cynicism had sunk deeper than I realized.

I reminded myself that I chose this path. Not to mention it was meaningful to the most meaningful person I had ever known. It felt like an obligation, but hopefully it would be more than just sightseeing.

Shaking off my skepticism, I sent my last work email before turning off my phone. Finding my seat and stuffing down the tidal wave of anxiety that came with air travel, I began my journey to Cody, Wyoming.

Cody is the only decent-sized city with an airport in the vicinity of Yellowstone National Park. However, the word "airport" is giving it a lot of credit. I was used to JFK and LaGuardia, which were huge international hubs. This was more like a long runway through the prairie with an air traffic control tower and a waiting room.

However, the people in the airport, and in the whole city for that matter, were incredibly friendly. It was a nice change of pace and the first notable difference from back home. I couldn't imagine that they had an influx of travelers in early September, but I wanted to visit the first destination on Charlie's list before the winter took Yellowstone off the board for a while.

My rental car ended up being the only vehicle left, a dayglow green Jeep Wrangler with big off-road tires. It was the loudest car color I'd ever seen and exactly the kind of ride Charlie would have picked.

I smiled, shaking my head. "Figures."

For what it's worth, Cody was a cool place. The whole city is nestled into this little gap at the foot of the Rockies, and everywhere you look, mountains dominate the horizon. Giant, towering granite peaks filled the sky higher than any skyscraper I'd ever seen. It was my first moment of awe since leaving home.

Sitting on the patio at my hotel, I pulled out Charlie's list for Yellowstone. There were some obvious items, like Old Faithful and Grand Prismatic. Toward the bottom were the words "Artist's Point" circled in red pen with a little star next to them and a note that read, "sit on the edge of the lookout."

A twinge of fear made my stomach tighten. This was a big step. I wrestled with this perpetual internal conflict between longing for more and fearing the unknown. Layer on top of that all the stages of grief. Emotionally, I was kind of a mess at that point.

Exhaling a deep breath of anxiety, I looked up at the horizon as the sun slowly set over the mountains to the west. The sky looked like it was on fire. Deep oranges, purples, and reds painted the skyline and reflected off the peaks of the mountains all around me. A tiny ember of adventure started to kindle in my heart. I snapped a picture of the sunset and sent it to Alicia and Samm with a note that read, "Arrived safe, and look, Charlie painted the sky for me."

Samm's response was a long line of shocked-face emojis, and Alicia sent back a huge heart with a text that read, "What a sunset!"

Leaning back in my chair and lacing my fingers together behind my head, I looked up at the sky and said, "OK, old friend, I'm here. First stop on the Inertia Hollins World Tour. I hope you're watching. Help me through this one—I need more than just the views."

⌘⌘⌘⌘

The next morning, I hit the road at ten of five. I read online that to beat the rush to the park's major attractions—you needed to get there early. It was dark when I left. The air was still crisp, but I felt a small surge of confidence as I rolled along the road in my bright-green Wrangler. It was a beautiful winding drive to the east entrance of Yellowstone. I took a selfie next to the sign.

"Proof of adventure," I said as I drove through the gate.

The first stop on my trip was the one that Charlie had circled in red, Artist's Point. I arrived at the overlook a few minutes before sunrise. The place was completely empty. The sun was still under the horizon but had just begun to heat up the sky. Gazing out over the edge, I was met with the sight of a giant canyon of yellow and orange and red rocks that flanked two sides of a busy river created by a massive waterfall at the far end. In the quiet and solitude of the morning, the only sound was the roaring lower Yellowstone falls cascading over the mountainside. The falls were loud and impressive, even a half mile away on the observation deck. There is not a more picturesque spot in the world to be alone with your thoughts.

"Feet over the wall," I said to myself, thinking of Charlie's note despite the clear signage against what I was about to do. He was never a "color inside the lines" type of person, and to honor him, I hopped up on the wall and let my feet dangle as I stared out into the canyon.

Sitting there, staring out at the huge valley before me, I was overcome with a flood of emotions. I broke down into tears, right on the spot. It was uncontrollable. It was like someone had uncorked a drain. Sobbing like a baby, gripping Charlie's list in my hand, I struggled to compose myself.

It didn't seem real. How could I be here *without him*? I was no adventurer. It all seemed so out of place. I expected to wake at any second and sit at the breakfast bar of our apartment with my best friend and recount the crazy dream I just had. But that moment never came. The breeze pushed against my face, forcing my tears to the sides of my cheeks, like an unseen hand attempting to wipe my face. I sat there, my emotions roiling inside me in stark contrast to the broad, powerful tranquility of my surroundings—a thunderstorm in paradise.

I sat there for a while until my solace was interrupted by some other early birds coming to grab a view. Not wanting to explain the damp cheeks and watery eyes, I decided it was time to move on. I hopped back into the Wrangler (I felt a little more rugged every time I got in it) and headed deeper into the park.

The remainder of the day was spent exploring the Norris Geyser Basin. Large pools of scalding liquid simmered across massive stretches of land that spanned the valley. The ground felt alive everywhere I walked. The air was thick with the scent of sulfur, sharp and ancient. Everything steamed and bubbled in a range of colors from bright white to a rust-colored orange. Every time a geyser would froth and spout into the sky, it felt like I wasn't on Earth anymore. I remember thinking that this is what the surface of Venus or Mercury must look like. I was beginning to understand—you don't just go see Yellowstone; *you feel it.*

The next morning, I set off to a different part of the park. First up was the Grand Prismatic Spring. Unfortunately, I hit a few delays. A few thousand, in fact. I decided to cut through Hayden Valley on my way there. This large grassland is a sub-alpine valley that sits in the middle of the park straddling the river that runs between the Yellowstone Lake and the falls area.

It's home to the park's locals, namely the enormous bison herds. I got stuck in what the rangers call a bison jam, where the herd decides to walk on the road, and tourists need to wait for them to pass. Bison, if you've never seen one in person, are massive. There's little anyone can do but just wait for them to pass; besides, the park is their home, and I was just a visitor.

The wait wasn't a total loss, though; it gave me plenty of time to reflect. I was really doing it. I was out in the world. I was on the adventure that Charlie had planned for us. It wasn't the panacea he had hoped it would be, at least not yet. I was still constantly afraid, constantly searching for that missing element in my life, and seeing all these spectacular geological formations without him was a very sharp and very private reminder of his absence. However, for the time being, the grief seemed to ebb a little knowing that he would have loved every minute of this (though I'm certain he would have tried to get a selfie with one of the bison, which probably would have gotten us both killed).

Grand Prismatic, when I finally arrived, certainly lived up to its name. It is a gigantic, sprawling, bubbling pool of liquid with concentric colored rings of almost every shade of the rainbow. There is a boardwalk that lets you get close to the spring itself, but it's hard to see the coloration unless you're up high above it. Luckily, there is an overlook close by on one of the hiking trails that heads up the mountains it sits next to. I wandered the boardwalk for a bit in the haze of the steam and bubbling noises, again feeling transported to another world. After that, I drove around to the trail head and made the quick hike up to the observation deck.

There was a tall, fit couple there about my age, dressed in hiking gear and baseball caps, leaning against the railing. The guy had a well-groomed beard of jet-black hair and heavily tattooed arms. The woman by his side had red hair in a French braid under her ball cap and an oversized Yellowstone hoodie. I decided to join them and take in the full view of the spring. It was nothing short of breathtaking. The world had a lot more to offer than crowded streets and traffic. I was starting to realize why Charlie had wanted us to see this.

"He sure would have loved this," the guy next to me said.

The comment startled me. Who was this guy? How did he know why I was here?!

"Excuse me?" I said, suddenly very nervous.

"Oh, sorry. I meant my son Max, he would have loved this," he replied.

Shaking off my suspicion, I said, "No, that's my bad. I don't know why I assumed you were talking to me. Why didn't you bring Max along with you?"

My words seemed to strike the two of them, and they glanced at each other with somber expressions before the woman turned to me and said, "Our son passed away two years ago."

Embarrassed and stammering, I tried to be considerate. "Oh my God, I'm so sorry. I didn't ... that was really dumb of me. I really do apologize."

"No harm done," the man said with a reserved melancholy look in his eyes. "Max's life was incredible but much too short. He was seven when he passed." The man's eyes were watering now as his wife squeezed his hand tightly and wiped a tear from her own eye. "He was hugely passionate about geology—volcanoes, earthquakes, geysers, and stuff like that. He always wanted to see the largest hot spring in the US, and we're honoring him by coming here."

I was stricken with empathy for them, having lost a child so soon in life. Also, I was anxiously curious about their story and how similar it was to mine. I was also at Yellowstone, at this very location, on this very day, to honor someone I had lost.

I couldn't help myself. I had to know. "I hate to pry, and if it's too painful, you don't need to answer, but what happened to Max?" Nervous that they would say a car accident, and this would be a full-blown glitch in the Matrix, I closed my eyes, fearing their response.

The woman replied somberly, "He was diagnosed with AML when he was six. Acute myeloid leukemia, one of the worst. Starts in the bones, spreads quickly to the blood. It's hard to treat, and we caught it late."

Incredibly, her answer made it worse. These poor parents. I shook my head. "That's horrible."

"It was," the man replied.

My gaze fell to the ground. "I'm so sorry. I don't know what to say."

He shrugged appreciatively. "It took a long time to heal or even consider making this trip. It still hurts, all the time, but it's grown bearable. Anyway, I'm sure you didn't climb this trail to hear about our son. What brings you to Yellowstone? Here on vacation?"

I was anxious to say anything, considering the similarities of our stories, but something tugging at my heart said this was not the time to withhold information.

Struggling to speak, I replied, "This will sound crazy, because it is, but I'm also here honoring someone that I lost. My best friend Charlie." The words caught in my throat, and my eyes began to water immediately. "He died in a car accident, but before he passed, he planned a trip for us to come here."

Their eyes grew as wide as golf balls. We stood there staring at each other in silence. I could see the tears welling up the woman's eyes again. The man stretched out his hand.

"August Peterson, and this is my wife, Katrina."

I shook both their hands quickly.

"Inertia Hollins. Nice to meet you, August & Katrina."

"Inertia?" Katrina asked. "Given or chosen?"

I looked at her confused. "I'm sorry?"

She giggled softly. "I'm sure no one's *ever* pointed out the uniqueness of your name. Did you choose it, or was it given to you?"

"Oh, given, actually."

"Even more interesting! Look Auggie, another member of the odd name club," she said, tugging on August's vest.

"Well, Inertia," August said confidently. "It seems like the universe has put us both on the same observation point in the same national park on the same day for the same reason. Maybe we were meant to run into each other. We are heading to Old Faithful after this to see what all the fuss is about. Are you on a tight schedule, or would you care to join us?"

I had to laugh—that was the last place on Charlie's list and my next stop. Maybe this trip *was* going to be more than just sightseeing.

"This just keeps getting weirder," I replied with a smile. "That's my next stop too."

August let out a loud, deep, full laugh. The kind of laugh that you'd expect from a strongman or a stonemason. "Well, of course it is! Excellent! A little company would be wonderful. Let's go."

⌘ ⌘ ⌘ ⌘

Old Faithful, the most famous geyser and biggest attraction at Yellowstone National Park, is surrounded by large parking lots, hotels, visitor centers, and a semicircle boardwalk full of benches for viewing this natural wonder. It is the busiest and most traveled part of the whole park by a wide margin. It's like a small town. The geyser itself is rather unassuming. It's basically a fifteen to twenty-foot hill of mud that reliably spouts boiling water thirty to fifty feet into the air about every two hours. The astoundingly consistent schedule it's kept since it's discovery in the 1870s is where it got its name, but if I'm honest, its appearance is a little underwhelming.

"That's Old Faithful?" Katrina said as we approached the benches surrounding the site.

August shrugged his broad shoulders and shook his head. "I guess so. Huh, I figured it would be ..."

"Taller?" I ventured with raised eyebrows.

"Yeah," they replied in unison.

August found a bench close to the edge of the viewing platform. "OK, well, I'm sure it's much cooler when it erupts. Let's have a seat and wait it out."

We sat down for a minute, and Katrina decided to run to the nearby gift shop.

"I'll be quick, I promise. I won't miss anything."

August and I leaned forward on the bench and gazed off at the steam rising from the land around us.

"So, Inertia, it looks like we have some time to kill. How about telling me the story of how you came to have such an unusual name? I'm sure it's interesting."

"Call me Ersch, most of my friends do; and I'm afraid it's not."

"Alright, Ersch, let's hear it. And you can call me Auggie."

I nodded. "Well, Auggie, my parents liked the word. Simple as that."

August slapped his hands on the bench in disbelief. "Nah! That can't be all of it!?"

I nodded again. "Afraid so."

He let out another loud bellow of laughter. It was kind of infectious. I started laughing with him.

"They just liked the word?!" he asked between gasps of air.

"Yup."

"Well, must have been a character builder growing up," he said, composing himself.

"It certainly was."

We sat for a bit, and I figured it was time to learn about him. "Your turn. Is August given or chosen?"

Taking a deep, measured breath, he leaned back as if recalling a distant memory. "Chosen. My given name was Justin, after my father. It was the only thing the coward ever gave me. He left us before I was old enough to form any memories of him. My mother said that he had a terrible drinking problem and that we would be better off without him. I hated my father for it, for leaving us like he did."

How could he just leave his son after naming him? I thought.

"My ma worked two, sometimes three jobs just to make sure she could afford the house and feed me. She never had a life of her own because when I was ten, my gram got sick and moved in with us. Ma had to care for both of us full time. So, as soon as I could work, I got a job to help cover our living expenses. Know many teens that helped their folks pay the bills?"

I shook my head, having grown up in a home with two loving parents my whole childhood. His situation was a little like Charlie's, having lost his father. But the Margolis family had a huge support system, something that seemed absent from Auggie's story. It sounded extremely hard, having to mature that quickly, almost like he was robbed of his childhood.

"No, Auggie. I don't."

"Yeah, well, that was my house. I grew up poor, but it made me strong. Anyway, my ma always loved the name August, but my father demanded that I was named after him. She sacrificed so much for me and gram that on my eighteenth birthday, I legally changed my name to August to both honor her and get closure on the father I never knew."

He fell silent for a minute, staring at the sky. I was struck by his story. Here was a man that had been abandoned by his father and lost his son, and still he had the grit and heart to laugh with me on a bench like a long-lost friend. It was good perspective. Everyone felt loss at some point in their lives. It wasn't just me.

"I've never shared that story with anyone but Katrina," he said, shaking his head. "You're surprisingly easy to talk to, Ersch. Has anyone ever told you that?"

"Yeah, my best friend used to say the same thing."

I shared the story of Charlie and his unexpected passing. He nodded, knowingly, when I described my nightmares, my apathy for the things I used to enjoy, and that feeling that there was a missing piece of myself that I couldn't seem to recover.

I leaned back. "He was just so important to me. So ... necessary. He accepted me as I was but also pushed me to be better. He was comfortable with my future—if you get what I mean."

He let out a heavy sigh. "Of course. He was part of who you are. He made you better, and now he's gone. And all anyone can say is, 'give it time,' when time is the most expensive thing you can imagine."

He was spot on. I put my elbows on my knees and propped my chin up with my hands. "I just wish there was a way through it faster. I wish there was some life hack for the grief."

Auggie looked down at his feet with a smile and nodded. "I can appreciate that. I was where you are about two years ago. The grief just buried me. There was a tension in my chest that felt like it would never leave. I looked for a quick fix, a cutoff from feeling the pain. I was a weaker man back then and still a lot like my father. I'm ashamed to say that I climbed inside a bottle for months to cope with the loss. It was too much. Even walking past Max's bedroom felt like a knife in my heart. I thought, surely, I could just dull the feeling. If I could just numb it long enough, it would go away. The irony is that the drinking made it worse. My shortcut backfired, big time. Had it not been for Katrina, forcing us both into therapy and me into rehab, we would never have made it."

His description was almost too close to home. I could feel every word he said like I was experiencing the pain myself, partially because I had. His coping mechanism was something I had considered many times to dull the pain. How different would my life have been if Alicia and Samm weren't there and instead I had leaned into a vice to deal with Charlie's death? It was like looking through a portal into an alternate reality.

"While I was in recovery, I learned a lot, Ersch. My biggest realization was that the shortcut is a lie. In fact, the shortcut is the longest path because even if somehow you make it work, you won't have developed enough character to keep what you gained."

I looked at him curiously. "What do you mean? I don't understand."

"It's like this—everyone's so eager to skip the hard part. Everyone's looking for a hack. In my experience, the quick fix is an illusion. It ain't just grief either. Wealth, health, fitness, marriage, parenting—it don't matter. The tough stuff in the middle is where all the magic happens. It's where you become the person that can handle what you want. The shortcut is a lie. Took me two years to figure that out, and I still screw it up."

August Peterson, another rare soul placed on my path to teach me about living better.

"That's profound, Auggie. Thank you for sharing."

He waved off the compliment dismissively. "Ah, but what the heck do I know, right? I'm just a recovering alcoholic with abandonment issues."

"Don't say that," I replied. "I'm an introverted finance bro that's barely seen outside the borders of Manhattan."

He put a strong arm around me and squeezed my shoulder. "I guess we're both a work in progress, Ersch."

I laughed. "No word of a lie, my friend."

Friend. I said the word freely and without hesitation. It gave me a moment of pause. I smiled, reaching into my shoulder bag for the journal Charlie had given me. I had started a small list of "wise things" that I had copied over from various people and places, like when I visited Myles that one time. I added a new line. *Auggie Peterson—Yellowstone— "The shortcut is a lie."*

No sooner had I put my journal back in my bag than Katrina came running up to us with three very large, very purple ice cream cones in her hands. She seemed positively giddy.

"Oh my God, Auggie! They had huckleberry soft serve in the gift shop! I couldn't resist. I got one for Inertia too. I hope that's OK? Do you eat dairy? Do you have any diet issues? That was careless of me. Are you even hungry? It's probably gluten free. I'm sorry, I should have asked first. I was just so excited that ..."

"Huckleberry? That's a real flavor?" I asked, confused.

The two of them shot me a look like I had sprouted a third ear.

"You've never tried huckleberry ice cream?!" Katrina said in disbelief.

Auggie leaned forward. "You weren't kidding about that barely-seen-the-borders-of-Manhattan thing. Ersch, it's the greatest. Pretty much a requirement of visiting the Northwest. They only grow in this area, and the locals put them in everything. Try it." He took one of the cones from Katrina and handed it to me.

I took a small lick off the side, "Wow! That's *really good.*"

Huckleberry is a rustic twist on a blueberry, with a little blackberry tartness. August was right—people put them in everything. Chocolate, jam, ice cream, candy, the list goes on. If it could be berry flavored, there's a huckleberry version of that in the Northwest.

About halfway through our ice creams, Old Faithful began to rumble and spout. A few minutes later, huge jets of steaming water shot high into the air. The ground rumbled under our seats. A large white steam cloud formed to one side that trailed off into the wind as onlookers cheered and took pictures. The three of us whooped and hollered as the famous geyser continued its show.

"OK, so that was kinda cool," I admitted.

"Totally worth the wait," Katrina replied.

I was planning on heading back to my hotel for the night, but Auggie insisted I have dinner with them. The three of us laughed and talked for hours. Katrina shared the story of how they met, and I told them about my friends and life back in New York. We talked at length about our late loved ones and shared stories and tears. We exchanged numbers so we could stay in touch, having quickly felt the bonds of friendship.

The day was full of unexpected events, but Yellowstone had one last surprise in store for me. I stopped by one of the larger visitor centers on my way out of the park to grab some huckleberry flavored food items for my friends. As I was leaving the visitor center, I noticed a large bronze plaque near the entryway.

It read, "This center was made possible by the generous donation of Myles Duncan McMasters."

I almost tripped and fell.

It couldn't be. I read the sign again. How was this possible!? My mind ripped back to my conversation with Myles. I remembered him talking about the quiet wealthy and their impact on the world. He had said something about passing average-looking people that had their names on plaques in ... I laughed in utter disbelief, repeating what he'd said, "... in every hospital, school, and national park in the nation!"

I took a picture of the plaque and sent it to Myles with a text that read, "Was this one of your investments?"

He replied a few minutes later with picture of him and Charlie's father standing in front of the sign when it was dedicated and a text that said, "What can I say, I'm a sucker for geysers."

The next morning, as the plane flew farther west to my next destination, I closed my eyes and pictured the massive canyons, waterfalls, wildlife, and hot springs of Yellowstone. It helped soothe my flight anxiety. I thought about August and Katrina and the wisdom and friendship they had shared. Maybe it was OK that I felt the way that I did. Maybe there really wasn't a quick fix for my nightmares like I wanted. Maybe this was that hard part in the middle where all the magic happened.

I had only been in Yellowstone a few days, but Yellowstone would live in me forever. Looking out the window at the puffy clouds below, my thoughts returned to Charlie.

Thank you, my friend. It was definitely more than just sightseeing. I can't wait to see what's next.

CHAPTER NINE

Truth in the Silence

"Huckleberries?"

"I'm telling you, Samm, they're amazing," I said as I propped my phone up on my luggage. "I'm serious. People in this part of the world put them in everything. I'm shipping you guys some dark chocolate and huckleberry bars, and I'll have jam to share when I get home."

Samm dove onto her couch with her phone still in her hands, causing the image on the screen to scramble a little. She brushed her hair back behind her left ear. "Sending a girl chocolate from the other side of the country—you sure are a charmer, Ersch."

I rolled my eyes at her obvious sarcasm. "Whatever, Kendricks. You can thank me later."

We talked for a few more minutes as I shared the logistics of the next location. This one was a little vague: "Explore the redwood forests." After that there was a short list of trails in the northern California area. Once I landed and rented another ride, I was on my way.

It was one of the prettiest drives I've ever taken. Even the baby trees were several stories tall, and they created the same canyon effect of the roads back home, except they were living things and not skyscrapers. The road seemed to always be shaded from the direct sun. Patches of moss and ferns grew abundantly on the forest floor. Light would pierce through the canopy in small slices, but only for an instant. There was an earthy druidic feel to the surrounding areas. It felt calming and ethereal.

I found a quiet little bed and breakfast practically in the middle of the woods. This place would become my home base while I explored the surrounding wilderness. They had a garden-style lawn filled with gnomes and other whimsical ornamentation. It was large enough for a few little sitting areas, where they had placed tables and chairs on decorative paver stones. It was cozy, and despite being the farthest distance I had ever traveled from home, I felt comfortable there.

Calling the gang and updating them on how things were going would have to wait because unfortunately (or maybe fortunately) the cell service was horrible. So, the cutting-edge tech in my pocket was little more than a camera for this excursion.

I sat down at one of the tables and reviewed the list of hiking trails that Charlie had detailed. There were five locations, all equally spread apart. Some I could not access with my vehicle, so there was a lot of hiking in my future.

One of the other guests at the bed and breakfast wandered into the garden and approached the table I was sitting at. She was a short, older woman with a soft stature and wiry, long, black hair with deep ringlets of silver in it. Tiny wooden and glass beads were dotted along tight braids here and there as she scooped up her hair and moved it from one shoulder to the other.

She wore a long skirt of greens and blues with multiple patterns, several dangling necklaces, and a bright linen shirt that contrasted with her dark skin and wild hair. Her hands and wrists were adorned with rings and bracelets made from multiple metals, threads, and different-colored stones. She smiled warmly with a face full of laugh lines from what I could only guess were decades of a life well lived. I said hello, and she replied in kind. Her voice was deep with age, and I immediately felt at peace when she spoke.

"Is this seat taken, young man?"

"No, please sit," I said, motioning to the chair next to me.

Feeling it somewhat necessary to be respectful, I got up quickly and tried to help her with her chair, but she waved me off with a chuckle.

"These old bones can manage just fine, but I appreciate the gesture."

She settled in, setting a small, dented thermos and terra-cotta mug next to her. She opened the thermos and poured out a thin, warm liquid that had a soothing aroma of lavender and some other wildflower that I couldn't quite place. I took a deep inhale as the steam wafted my way.

"That smells amazing," I said as I exhaled.

"Chamomile and lavender. My favorite. I apologize for not bringing mugs for the both of us, but I didn't expect company in the garden this early." She stretched out her hand. "Jamala Smith, but most folks just call me Jay."

I shook her hand, remarking at what a firm grip she had. "My name's Inertia." I had grown so accustomed to people asking questions or reacting surprised after I told them my name that I just readied myself for the typical list of inquiries.

She nodded softly. "I like that. What brings you to North Cali, Inertia? Going to see the trees?"

"I am," I said, surprised.

She continued, "Well then, you're in for a treat. First time, I take it?" I nodded. "Even better. They're very special, these redwoods," she said, looking off into the forest.

She sipped her tea and exhaled. "They slow down time for me, help to quiet my mind. Life seems better in the trees. Good perspective on how small my problems really are." She chuckled a little. "If something like a redwood can grow dozens of feet wide and hundreds of feet tall and shrug off a forest fire—well then, my troubles seem pretty trivial."

Jamala seemed to emanate a relaxing energy. I couldn't quite place my finger on it, but it seemed impossible to feel any of my typical social anxiety or worry sitting next to her.

"Has anyone ever told you that you've got a pretty chill vibe?"

She winked at me quickly. "Well, I don't know if they used those words, but yeah. And you, kiddo, if you'll pardon my boldness, seem a little out of place. If I had to guess, I'd say you live in a big city—East Coast? DC or Boston? Maybe the Big Apple? If you're here for the redwoods, my guess is that it's on vacation. Bucket list type thing?"

She was alarmingly intuitive. I was very out of place. The designer clothes and obviously rented car were probably a dead giveaway. So, I opted for a short version of the story, not wanting to reopen the wound.

"Yeah, something like that. A friend of mine passed away a few months back. He wanted to come here with me, and some mutual friends of ours convinced me to take the journey in his memory."

Jamala nodded slowly, taking the time to absorb what I had said before replying. She sipped her tea again.

"He was close to you then, this friend of yours?"

"He was."

The words felt heavy as I spoke them. Jamala sat in contemplation, not responding right away. She opened her thermos again and poured a little more tea. We sat there quietly in the garden, and it was like the world settled around us. The breeze softened. The birds grew silent.

"You were right to come, then," she said after a long pause. "You'll find what you're looking for in the woods, but you'll need to quiet your mind. I meditate. Ever try it?"

I shrugged. "Me? Meditation? Nah, I don't think I could handle it. Couldn't stand the silence."

She turned her head, her brows furrowed into a curious expression, like she was examining me. "Why are you afraid of silence, Inertia?"

"Because it only tells the truth."

The response was almost automatic, like a defense mechanism. I clenched my jaw after the words escaped my mouth. My eyes began to tear up. So much for not reopening the wound.

"A wise response for one as young as yourself. Maybe there's a gift in there you haven't explored yet. Maybe you can't see it through all the distractions and grief. Meditation might be exactly what you need."

My old familiar self-doubt rose up to defend against Jamala's suggestions that I might be anything more than average. Almost reflexively, I replied, "Well, maybe you don't know me well enough. I'm nothing special."

She clicked her tongue loudly. "Young man, that's a terrible attitude! Now, I can see you're hurting. That's obvious. You know, I saw a picture a few weeks back of a marble man that was chiseling himself out of the block of marble that he was made from. The message is that most of us won't change for the better because we forget we are both the marble and the sculptor. Real change does require some pain and suffering. It's clear to me that your trip out here has been bittersweet and that you're coping with some pain and suffering."

My shoulders slumped with a heavy sigh. She grabbed my hand, squeezed it tightly, and continued. "That's good, honey, that's good! That means you're growing. That pain you're feeling is the chisel. You're carving the marble right now, and that means you're doing right by your late friend."

I looked over at her as a tear dripped off the end of my chin.

"Do an old woman a favor and try to find that silence you're so afraid of. Maybe the truth it has to tell you is something you need to hear. Find yourself a place in the woods that feels right. You'll know it when you're there. When you feel it, just have a seat, right where you are. Then close your eyes, take a few deep breaths, and just listen and trust. Will you do that for me, dear?"

I nodded, wiping my eyes. "I will."

She released my hand and sat back in her chair. "Good boy."

Jamala took another sip of her tea and looked up at the trees. After a bit, she got up from her chair, nodded at me with a smile, and said, "Enjoy yourself, kiddo. Been nice chatting with ya."

She walked off into the garden, thermos and mug in hand, until she passed by a large rosebush and walked out of sight around the side of the building. I sat there a while, thinking about what she had said, and a funny feeling came over me. Despite being alone in the garden, it felt like I was being watched. However, it wasn't sinister; it was compassionate, like the way a parent would look at their sleeping child.

That was the first and last time I ever saw Jamala Smith. There was no record of her ever being a guest at the bed and breakfast, and neither the owners nor any of the other guests saw anyone that day that matched her description. Thinking back on our brief conversation, it feels like a dream. I know that sounds unbelievable. However, to this day, I'm still unable to say for sure if she was a real person, if I imagined her, or if she was the soul of the forest itself, sent to push me along this path.

৯৯৯

The redwoods of northern California are possibly the most impressive living things I have ever seen, and perhaps will ever see, in my life. The first few hikes I went on were incredible. Towering giants rose from the forest floor like ancient guardians of their surroundings. I paced around one tree that sat in a solitary grove, and it took me close to forty-five steps to walk around the trunk. Their barks were thick and furrowed, the flares of their roots as thick as bridge cables. Everywhere I looked, a compounding sense of awe overtook me.

I remember walking by a redwood that had fallen and had been cut widthwise so as to not obstruct the path. The slice exposed the rings of the tree so you could easily count them. I counted thirty rings, a little over the length of my entire life, and the depth of that span of time was barely noticeable compared to the rest of the tree rings. It must have been close to a thousand years old when it fell. Imagine living over a millennium?

Like Jamala had said, it really did put my problems into perspective. Most of the members of these groves were already old when the Roman Empire fell. Their canopy reached into the clouds before Joan of Arc was born, before the Samurai, before the first stone of Machu Picchu was laid. Consider the breadth of that much time. It was a deeply humbling experience. This forest commanded reverence.

The longer and farther I walked, the more entranced I became. The trees were staggeringly large and grew incredibly close together. It seemed impossible that they didn't somehow communicate with one another through their root systems. In fact, the longer I stayed in the forest, the more I began to feel like it was just one large organism, attached underground in ways humans couldn't see or understand.

It's hard to spend any time walking amongst the redwoods without feeling a deep connection to nature. I remember feeling so fortunate that I had the opportunity to walk among these age-old sentinels. To think they had always been a simple plane ride away. Here I lived for almost three decades in the busiest corner of the Northeast, convinced that it was the center of the universe. The quiet, stalwart nature of the trees stood as clear evidence that there were bigger and better things out there than the streets of New York. Manhattan might always be my home, but in the company of the redwoods, my introversion started to wither, and I felt called to experience more of the other amazing places the world had to offer me.

⤚⤙⤚⤙

On the last day, on my last hike, something remarkable happened. I was about a mile down the trail, and I came upon a huge fallen redwood that had crashed into another and caused this large pile of huge logs and splinters. It must have been a terrifying sight to behold, trees of that size slamming into one another and falling over. Now it just made for a cool spot to explore. I clambered up onto the trees and walked across the top of the pile, dodging branches as large as regular trees as I moved slowly along the length of the trunks.

I came across a spot where the splintered remains of one tree had fallen directly between two others, creating a bit of a bridge. I noticed a small carving there. It was an elaborately etched vine that surrounded a deep carving of the letter "J" in calligraphy.

"No way," I spoke to the open air. The forest seemed to fall utterly still at my discovery. I recalled Jamala's words, "You'll know the place." She also said that most people called her Jay, and here I was looking down at a detailed carving of her first initial. I looked around for a second, waiting for the hidden camera crew to pop out and tell me that this was all staged. I pinched my side hard, half expecting to wake up. It seemed too coincidental for it not to have been planted. However, after a few minutes of waiting, no film crew emerged from the bushes, and I obviously wasn't sleeping.

Maybe this isn't a coincidence, I thought.

"Well, I did promise I would try," I said with a shrug, pulling off my backpack and getting comfortable on the log.

I sat there for what seemed like forever—mind busy with the logistics of my hike back to my lodging, my flight home, the details of returning the car. I awkwardly crossed my legs one way, then the other, fiddling with the positioning of my hands in my lap. I opened my eyes, then closed them again. Opened them slowly, then closed them tightly. I adjusted again, tried to sit on my heels and then on my bag until finally I got frustrated and threw my bag to the side.

It felt like a big hoax, like I had set myself up for failure—finding any little piece of connection into a long chain of confirmation bias to make it seem like I was being guided to this spot. That carving on the tree could have meant anything. Suddenly, that hard, cynical city boy I had been repressing during the trip simmered up to the surface again.

Shouting up into the canopy, I said, "This is stupid! There are no answers here! What did I expect?! This isn't some movie where the hero's mentor appears out of the woods like a spirit guide! No one is coming to save me! He's gone! He's never coming back! What good could this possibly do!?"

I felt more alone then than I ever have before. Not only was I away from familiar places, but I was also isolated from any other human I knew. Even amid all that remarkable beauty, everything felt like a big waste, like nothing would ever return to the way it was. My head fell into my hands, and I broke down. I tried my best to compose myself, but the emotions came at me like a wave, and all I could do was hang on and wait for it to pass. I took a few deep breaths and wiped my eyes. I tilted my head back against the tree, looking up at the canopy again. I couldn't understand why it still hurt so much. It felt like the pain would go on forever.

There must be a way through this, I thought.

I checked my phone—still no service. The crutch it had become offered no solace to me here. There was little to distract me from the silence. I opened my picture folder, scrolling through shots of August and Yellowstone. Bison, geysers, and the bright-green Wrangler. I kept scrolling through old pics of Charlie and the crew back home. Sunsets, treetops, the Manhattanhenge, the ladies all decked out for my birthday. There were selfies of Charlie and me at dinner, at the speakeasy afterwards, mere hours before ...

Then it hit me, the guilt.

It blasted me unexpectedly, like a firehose. It swamped my senses. It was overwhelming. Had I been repressing it all this time? Thoughts flooded into my brain, a tide of contempt, self-loathing, and regret. If only I hadn't rushed to catch our ride before the light changed. If I had waited a few seconds, if I had been more aware, if I had just paid more attention, maybe I'd be sharing this journey with him instead of facing it alone. It was a cruel realization. I wasn't just mourning; *I felt responsible.*

I remember breaking the silence of the forest with a loud scream. Emptying my lungs into the air, my voice reverberated off the stalwart behemoths as they stood in silent witness. I rubbed the small scar above my temple from the car windshield. The loneliness was crippling.

The forest responded with more silence. Almost like it was waiting for something. I took a few more deep breaths and resolved to try again. I put my phone away, picked up my bag, and sat back down against the tree. I slowly closed my eyes, sniffled a little, and let out a deep exhale. Taking another long deep breath, I let it out slowly. My mind drifted a bit, but I just kept trying to come back to the next breath. I kept that up for a few more minutes, and the wind began to stir a little.

I could hear the trees swaying hundreds of feet above me. It sounded like a hushed conversation, like the limbs were sharing secrets. A tingling sensation started at my shoulders and then worked its way up to my ears. My neck and back relaxed, and I took another deep breath. My focus seemed to blur a little, and the sensation of sitting on the log seemed to soften a bit. I took another deep breath. My arms, legs, and sides began to feel lighter. I took another deep breath. The wind picked up a little more. I took another deep breath.

It was then, alone in the depths of the redwood forest, isolated from any other humans by miles, that I heard the truth I had never realized I needed or perhaps was too afraid to accept. Sitting in that ageless wood, mustering whatever meditative ability I had, the clear and concise voice of my best friend Charlie entered my head and said:

"It's not your fault."

CHAPTER TEN

The Second
Law of Motion

The flight back home felt like a time warp. I was on the plane, but it didn't really feel like I was on the plane. My mind was still stuck in the forest, replaying those four simple words in my head. It was clear as day, like Charlie himself was sitting next to me. It shook me to my core. It was almost too much at once—the realization that I was still holding onto guilt and the voice in my ears that so clearly affirmed I didn't need to.

The captain's voice came over the plane's speaker system signaling that we were beginning our descent to JFK. I snapped out of my trance for a second to stare out the window. The darkness stretched out everywhere until the shine of the city pierced the blackness. My vacation days were used up for the moment, so I would spend the holiday season back home and head back out again in spring to finish Charlie's list.

It was late. When I descended the escalator toward the baggage claim, I spotted the bright smiles of two familiar faces. Alicia and Samm were standing there waving at me. Samm was holding a cardboard sign like a chauffeur that read, "Science Class." I shook my head.

"You just couldn't resist, could you, Kendricks?" I said with a grin.

When I got clear of the escalator, Samm dropped her sign and leapt at me, wrapping her legs around my waist and her arms around my neck. I didn't expect such a warm welcome, and I almost fell over.

"You're back!" she said, squeezing me.

"Ugh, I missed you too," I said as I strained to stand.

Alicia rubbed her hand on my side. "Alright, love, best hop off the poor man before you injure him."

Samm jumped down and punched me in the arm in her usual fashion. I had become very close to them. They were basically family. Alicia was like that cool mature cousin that you always looked up to, and Samm, well she had become the little sister I never knew I needed.

Picking her cardboard sign back up, we headed to the baggage claim. "That chocolate you sent us, holy cow, amazing! I'm obsessed! We ordered a case!"

I laughed. "I told you it was good. You should try the ice cream."

The two of them, eyes wide, turned and said in unison, "They make ice cream?!"

We grabbed my bags and headed back to my apartment. On the trip home, I shared a bit about my adventures. We talked about the brightly-colored Jeep, the fun young couple I met in Yellowstone, and the kind old woman that talked with me in the redwoods. Alicia remarked that I was starting to sound a little like Charlie, having met new friends everywhere I went.

"Maybe travel was exactly what you needed to come out of that shell a bit more," she continued. "I think Charlie knew exactly what he was doing, planning these trips to get you out of New York."

It caught me off guard because there was some truth in her comments. I did meet some interesting people, and I was considerably more sociable than usual. The thought of meeting strangers didn't cause that pit of anxiety in my guts like it usually did.

"Bet you had a lot of time to sort out your feelings," Samm said.

"You don't know the half of it, Samm. I had the weirdest thing happen while hiking in the redwoods. Like, bordering on supernatural."

I relayed the story of my time hiking amongst the giants, my frustrating attempts at meditation, and the revelations about the guilt I was still holding onto. Then, I told them about finally settling my mind and hearing Charlie's voice in my ears.

"It was like something out of a movie, Samm. It was unbelievable. I thought about it the whole way home. It made me realize how hard I am on myself sometimes. But I guess before you can fix a thing, you gotta figure out what's wrong, you know?"

In my journey through life, I periodically exposed shortcomings about myself that caused me a lot of undue pain and suffering. This was a big one. In addition to rarely taking credit when it was due or compliments when they were given, I blamed myself for practically everything.

I looked up from my moment of self-reflection to lock eyes with Alicia in the rear-view mirror. I could see the small line of a tear rolling down her cheek.

"I'm so proud of you, Inertia," she said.

When we got to my apartment, the two of them hopped out and grabbed my bags from the trunk, and we had a quick friend-huddle.

Stepping back into my place after a few weeks away was a welcome sight. I took a deep breath and dropped my things, sifting through the pile of junk mail and turning on some music. I wandered to the window, then to the fridge, forgetting that I had emptied it before leaving.

"Take out it is," I said with a frown.

I walked around the apartment looking at pictures and keepsakes that we had collected over the years in the way an art gallery visitor would admire paintings in a museum. Things felt different now. I had the budding roots of some self-confidence and was finally starting to formulate a plan for my life. I knew I wanted to live on my own terms, and that a career in finance would always be a golden cage. Maybe it would be worth riding out for another year or two, but even that felt incomplete. As for what I'd do instead, well, that was still a mystery I was trying to solve.

One thing I was certain of was the need to get on with my life. The apartment had become a mausoleum for Charlie Margolis the Third, but I reminded myself that Inertia Hollins still lived here too. Sifting through a bunch of Charlie's old things, I made a "keep" and a "toss" pile. The cards, letters, and sympathy reminders that still cluttered the breakfast bar were bagged up and thrown away. I used one of the shelves in his room to condense all his social media awards as well as my favorite pictures of the two of us. About a half hour in, my food arrived, and I ate and sorted late into the evening. It was immeasurably cathartic.

There were trinkets and pictures that grabbed at my heart and made me cry. There were also just as many that made me burst into laughter (like the keys to the steamroller). It made me realize that the process of remembering wasn't always a look back in sorrow. It could also be a look forward in joy.

How could I live in a way that would make him proud? I wondered.

It was important to maintain his memory, but I also knew he'd be mad at me for living the way I had been, all sad and wounded. He had said as much with his last words to me.

Under the surface, I was still a shy introvert, but that had started to change. There was still a nagging sense of incompleteness in my mind, and my self-worth was still far from healthy, but that had started to change as well. If I was going to somehow make it on my own and find this missing piece of myself, I couldn't get distracted. I knew in the morning I would return to the grind of the finance world. It took a significant emotional event to shake me from the slumber of my life once, and I didn't want to repeat the lesson.

⁂

The doors to the elevator parted, and there was Leonidas the bronze lion, stalwart as ever, staring back at me from the entrance to the firm.

"Morning, big guy," I said as I patted the statue on the head.

I was greeted with smiles and updates about what had happened while I was away. The muscle memory of grabbing my *Metropcicle* mug (that I stole from Charlie's first merch run) and filling it with hot coffee was automatic. Taking a seat at my desk, I logged back into my accounts, started my music, opened the same six websites we used to monitor the markets, and spread them across my multiple screens in the same pattern I always had. It was mechanical and subconscious, and it scared me a little.

Just like that, I thought to myself, fighting a flash of apprehension.

It was so easy to fall back into complacency, to accept that settle-for life. Most of my day was just habit. People wonder why time seems to fly by so quickly. Maybe it's because we tend to relive the same year seventy-five times and attempt to call that a life.

However, falling back into the routines of my life is exactly what happened. I was tolerating my situation but not trying to improve it.

It was like the story of the dog sitting on the nail. Sure, he's howling about how much the nail hurts, but he's grown so used to the pain that he doesn't get up and move somewhere else. It isn't until the pain of the nail becomes greater than his fear of change that he finally gets up and does something about it.

I'm a little ashamed to say that after a few weeks home that's exactly where I was. Sitting on the nail, for months. All my problems still existed, and Charlie's list remained unfinished. I quietly longed for more adventure, but the conveniences of urban life were a strong anesthetic for my wanderlust.

Although, despite the slump I found myself in, I had promises to keep, and that simple thought was enough force to start gaining speed again. It was also all the universe needed to poke me in the chest and remind me of my tasks undone.

❦❦❦

It was a gray spring Tuesday, and the deep cold of the winter was finally behind us for another year. The office had moved to a hybrid work environment, and we were only expected to be in the office three days a week. I decided this was a good day to stay home. It had rained on and off for the better part of the month, making everything feel damp and gloomy. Perfect time for a trip to the local coffee shop for a fancy hot beverage, a comfy chair, and some free Wi-Fi. I walked onto the street and opened my umbrella, shuffling into the flow of people on the sidewalks. About halfway there, I could smell the fresh coffee as it filled the path in front of me.

I opened the door to my favorite local place with a deep inhale, dropped my umbrella in the bucket at the door, and wiped my feet on the doormat. This place had a lot of character. Aside from always smelling fantastic, there was lots of odd furniture and walls full of books, trinkets, and funny artwork. Ornamental pendant lights hung all over the place, covering the shop in a warm yellow glow.

The barista, Lucian, was a friend of mine. His family owned the place, and he was in his third year working toward a law degree at PACE university. They lived in Nolita. The shop was packed, but despite how busy he was, his face lit up with a big smile at the sight of me.

"Inertia Hollins, well hello, my friend! It's been some time! So good to see you!"

"Hey, Lucian. Business looks good," I said, nodding toward all the people seated about the shop.

He clapped his hands together excitedly. "Not bad, right!? Things have really picked up lately. So, what can I get you today? Same as usual, or are you feeling adventurous?"

I was feeling the opposite of adventurous but figured coffee was a safe place to start turning that ship around.

"Let's go with adventurous," I said hesitantly.

"Excellent! We just got in this great Costa Rican blend, smooth as silk. I'll grind it for you fresh!"

He busily moved around the other staff, prepping my drink and assisting with other orders. I turned quickly, not realizing there was someone getting up from a table, and we collided, spilling her drink on the floor.

"Oh my gosh, I'm so sorry," I said, immediately grabbing napkins and helping to clean up the mess. The woman looked up at me with these intense aquamarine eyes. She had fair skin and was a little shorter than me with raven hair that was pulled back in a tight ponytail. She was stunningly beautiful.

She shook her head and said, "Ah, don't worry about it. It's just a cup of coffee. *Don't be sad for me.*"

Her words struck me like a bolt of lightning. I froze, staring at her wide-eyed. "What did you just say?!"

She recoiled a little. "Uh, it's just a cup of coffee?"

I shook my head, dumbstruck. "No, after that."

"Umm, don't be sad for me? I mean, really, it's not a big deal, not like it can't be ..."

Her words trailed off into a haze of rambling sounds. For a few seconds, I could barely breathe. Funny how we think we're getting over something and then a song or picture, or in this case a phrase, will drag us back into all our unresolved feelings. The words hit me like a hypnotic suggestion. It was like a show you'd see in Las Vegas where a planted phrase makes someone behave erratically, except this phrase paralyzed me. I stood there, unable to say or do anything.

After a little bit of this, the woman looked at me, worried. "Uh, are you OK?" she asked, seeing the shocked expression on my face. She looked around quickly. "Seriously, it was just a coffee. Are you alright? You look like you just got the worst news of your life."

I snapped out of my momentary shock. "Uh, yeah, sorry again. I just remembered something that caught me a little off guard"—which was mostly true— "I'm so sorry. That was so careless of me. Can I get you a replacement for the coffee I spilled?"

"That would be nice," she said, wiping the front of her coat.

I took a breath to settle my mind and could feel the awkwardness of the exchange seeming to get worse instead of better. I broke the uncomfortable silence with the first thing that came to mind.

"So, what brings you out today?" I grimaced tightly, shaking my head. "Oh God, my bad, that sounded awful. Here I am trying to make things less awkward, and I made them worse, didn't I?"

She nodded. "Yeah, you kinda did."

I sighed heavily. "I'm terribly sorry. Let me start over." I took a deep breath and reached out a hand. "My name's Inertia Hollins."

She shook my hand. "Inertia? Really? That's an interesting name."

I rolled my eyes. "You're the first person to notice."

She raised an eyebrow with a snarky grin. "Sure I am."

She looked out the window as if scanning the crowd for someone. "To answer your question, I was here to meet someone, but he's about an hour late and isn't answering my texts. First time I've been ghosted. It's a bummer. I was starting to like this guy."

She shrugged, seeming to cast off the situation. I shrugged back, doing my best to make her feel better. "Well, I don't know you, but I'd bet it's his loss."

She smiled, and I relaxed a little more.

"That's sweet of you to say. Sometimes I'm not so sure," she replied.

"I don't believe that for a second," I said, feeling a little more confident. "You seem like a great person."

"Based on what?" she asked. "How I look?"

I blushed immediately, looking down at my shoes. "Really am batting a thousand today, aren't I?"

She laughed, shaking her head. "Sure are."

Lucian whistled from behind the counter. I turned to see him holding two large cups of coffee. He winked at me with a little nod in the woman's direction, almost like he was silently egging me on. I turned around and handed her the replacement cup. She thanked me and took a small sip, sitting back down at her table. There was something about her that drew me in. It wasn't just her looks, though she was stunning. It was almost like she was tuned to a frequency I couldn't hear until we made eye contact. Despite risking further embarrassment, I felt the need to talk with her more.

"Is that seat taken?" I asked, sheepishly pointing at the chair opposite her.

"Wow, seriously?" she replied.

"Yeah, sorry. That was really forward of me. You probably don't want ..."

"No, sit," she said, interrupting me. "Today's already been a huge let down; how much worse could it get?"

I fumbled with my chair and sat down uncomfortably, trying to make small talk. "This place makes the best coffee, doesn't it?"

She nodded curtly. "Yep."

I nodded back in agreement. "Shame it's been raining so much." The comment felt forced and uncomfortable. So, I sipped my coffee and apologized again for my blunder. Anyone viewing the conversation would probably have been embarrassed *for me*.

She laughed, shaking her head, "OK, I need to know—you aren't, like, a serial killer, right? Like, you aren't grooming me or anything because we're surrounded by witnesses, and I will scream if you try something."

The comment crushed me. My shoulders fell, and I gave her the most honest smile I could manage.

"No, ugh, farthest thing from it. I'm just an awkward guy in a coffee shop, trying to make amends. My apologies. Never was any good in the people skills department," I said humbly.

We locked eyes again, and her intense stare seemed to soften a little. She tilted her head like she had seen something curious. I stood to leave, mortified at the whole situation.

"I should go," I said, defeated.

As I turned to exit, she grabbed my hand, preventing me. "No, sit back down. Please."

Surprised and relieved, I took my seat, and she looked deep in my eyes like she was searching for something.

"Tell me, Inertia, do your friends believe your smile or your eyes?"

"What? What do you mean?" I asked, confused. She looked at me with this tender, disarming gaze that drew me in further.

"Your smile and your eyes," she continued. "They tell very different stories. I wonder which one is true?"

"I ... uh ... well," I stammered, not knowing how to respond.

"It's OK, just a passing thought," she replied.

"I'm sorry, I didn't catch your name," I said, trying to recover.

Not breaking eye contact, she said, "You apologize a lot."

"Wow, what a weird name," I said sarcastically. "And I should know—I'm a bit of an authority on the subject."

This made her giggle, both a welcome sound and a huge relief.

"My name's Violet Royce."

"Royce?" I asked. "Like the ..."

She shook her head. "I wish. I certainly wouldn't be here if that were the case."

"Well, I'm glad it's not," I replied, feeling a little bolder.

"Why?" she asked cynically. "So, you didn't have to spill someone else's coffee?"

Her response was like a punch in the gut. I felt like I was continuously gaining traction just to flounder again.

"Yeah, my bad, I'm a bit clumsy sometimes."

"There you go again, apologizing," she replied.

I shook my head. "Yeah, maybe we should change the subject. Do you live in the area?"

She nodded. "I do, and how about you, Inertia? Is the city home?"

"It is. I live about eight blocks from here."

There was a pause. She smiled a little, almost like she was surprised by something. I could feel this strange magnetism develop. It was like the silence between us was full instead of empty. There was a kinship that seemed present, just under the surface, like an echo or a memory. Her expression suggested she felt it too, like instinct or resonance.

She exhaled awkwardly, breaking the quiet between us. "So, got any plans for the springtime? Going anywhere fun?"

I was grateful for the question. "Well, my birthday is in a few months. There are a few places I planned on going, but I'm not sure."

She looked at me inquisitively. "What's stopping you?"

I shrugged. "I don't know if I'm ready for more adventures yet, if that makes any sense."

She shook her head. "No. It doesn't," she said with a laugh. "I travel as much as I can. My parents both died before my twenty-third birthday, and they both regretted not seeing more of the world. I do everything I can to make sure that's not one of my regrets when I die. None of us know how much time we have. I'd book my next trip today if I were you. Waiting for the right moment is stupid. My plan is to spend as much of my time as possible on a journey instead of at a job. We were made for so much more."

She made a good point, especially considering the events of the last year. Life gave no assurances. It was also a stark reminder of the commitments I had made after returning from the redwoods. Commitments I was doing a terrible job at keeping.

"I have no idea why I just shared all that with you," she said. The quiet attraction seemed to settle back in between us. She looked at me and sipped her coffee again. Standing up quickly, Violet walked to Lucian's counter and grabbed a pen. Pulling her receipt from her pocket, she began to write something. Holding up the receipt, she said, "This is my number. If you can make it a few more minutes without apologizing for something, I'll let you have it. I don't buy into all that fate crap, but there's something about you, Inertia, and today has been too weird not to take a chance."

Startled by her boldness, I shifted in my chair, accidentally kicking her in the shin. She winced in pain.

"Oh my God, I'm so sorry!" I spouted, almost involuntarily.

She clenched her teeth and crumpled up the receipt. "So much for that idea."

Panicking, I stumbled over my words. I felt like a fool. She stood up from her seat and rubbed her leg. There was a short silence between us.

"Violet, I ..."

"It's OK, really. Listen, I'm gonna go. Thanks for the coffee."

I watched her walk out the door. She turned and looked back at me with those intense blue eyes. A curious grin formed on her face, like she was thinking about staying. Then, she winked at me and raised her cup as she turned and disappeared into the crowd.

Collapsing back into my chair, Lucian looked over at me, eyes full of anticipation.

I shook my head somberly.

He laughed. "Don't worry, my friend! She's a regular like you. I'm sure you'll bump into her again. Ha! Maybe not literally next time!"

His jab at me was friendly but stung more than expected. I spent the next hour at the coffee shop wallowing in self-pity, thinking up all these great things that I should have said to make her stay. I searched social media for anyone with her name, and she either didn't have accounts or kept them private.

"What a train wreck," I said to myself on my walk home. "I just let her vanish into the streets of a rainy Tuesday!"

I opened the apartment door and slammed it closed. Walking to my laptop, I logged back into the work server. It was a slow day on the markets. Snapping my laptop closed in frustration, sitting there in a fog of embarrassment and remorse, I looked down at my desk.

Charlie's list of destinations sat there patiently, unfazed by this season of procrastination. Violet was right. Even though I had totally blown my chances of ever getting to know her better, she was right. Tomorrow was a promise to no one. Speaking of promises, it was time to start keeping mine. Opening my laptop back up, I pulled up a search engine and set about the task of planning my next trip. It was time for the next adventure.

CHAPTER ELEVEN

Salt Life

Charlie loved pie. It was his favorite dessert in the whole world. Of all the pies that he loved, key lime was the undisputed king. Periodically, he would buy them from local bakeries and then stand at the kitchen counter with a spoon and eat the whole thing in one sitting without saving me a crumb. It's likely he would have shared his toothbrush before he let anyone have even a morsel of his key lime pie.

It was his ultimate comfort food. The speed at which he consumed it was a good indicator of how well his day had gone. If he savored it and ate it slowly, it had been a good day, like when his channel broke five million subscribers. If he tore through it like a starving bear, it had been a bad day, like the day we buried his father.

So, when the Florida Keys appeared on his list, it didn't surprise me at all. He had laughed about one day paying a visit to where key limes are grown to see if we could find that ultimate slice of his very favorite food. His list for this location was simple: paddleboards, snorkeling, mangroves, and pie.

I flew into Miami airport and rented a convertible for the trip. They gave me this zippy little two-door soft-top Mini Cooper. It was hunter green with a tan leather interior. It was incredibly fun to drive. I had a blast chasing sports cars down the highway.

On another adventure. It was like stepping into a story where the ink was still wet and the map was half-drawn. Everything pulsed with possibility. My thoughts drifted as the warm ocean breeze blew against my skin. My birthday was around the corner, as was the first anniversary of Charlie's passing, the two events now indelibly joined in a bittersweet ball of emotions. It seemed ironic how fate would sometimes briefly spoil important days with the memory of things I'd like to forget.

When I got to Key Largo, I was expecting massive resorts and miles of white sand like you'd find on any of the famous coastal beaches around the nation, but this was nothing like that. I drove past all these tiny communities with one-story homes and coastal inlets where everyone had a driveway and a dock. Everywhere I saw funky golf carts and sun-bleached beachy homes that crowded the winding roads of these neat little communities of people that chose to make life a full-time vacation.

Snorkeling was the first item on my list. There's no coral on the mainland, so you need to take a boat out to the marine sanctuaries to see any of the sea life the area is known for. I settled on an outfitter that came highly recommended by a bunch of locals and booked a slot for the following day.

Stopping at one of the state parks just before sunset, I grabbed a lobster roll for dinner from a street-food vendor set up nearby. It was almost worth the trip on its own—a warm, comforting bun with a heaping portion of chilled lobster, a hint of lemon zest and sea salt served with coleslaw on the side. It was one of those meals that evokes that lazy, sun-drenched island vibe.

Speaking of sun, a Florida Keys sunset should be on everyone's bucket list. The sky explodes into this tapestry of molten gold, burnt orange, and coral pinks that melt into soft lavender and shades of indigo. Tiny little wisps of clouds catch light like brushstrokes on a canvas, drifting carefree over the turquoise ocean.

Why didn't I do stuff like this sooner? I thought, watching it all unfold.

⸜⸝⸜⸝

I walked excitedly to the dock the next morning and was met by a tall guy about my age with dark skin and short, dyed dreadlocks that sprouted out of his topknot. He had a *very* thick Jamaican accent and spoke in his native dialect called Patois (Pah-twa), which took some getting used to. He introduced himself as Patrice Thompson, saying that he would be my captain for the day. I didn't want to be late, so I hurried down the dock at my full NYC street pace.

"Good day to yuh, Mistah," he said with a smile, "Mash up yuh brakes, ya? Be no need for rushing. Grab a seat on mi boat. We be waiting on a few more."

The boat quickly filled with passengers. Patrice motioned to his crew of hopeful snorkelers. "Small up yuh self now. Yuh be irie, nobody gonna bite yuh."

We took his boat out to Grecian Rocks off the coast of Key Largo—a shallow reef with brightly colored coral and lots of tropical fish. He handed each of us our gear, and we dove in the calm teal waters. I swam along, looking around at the expansive aquatic habitat. Staring down at all the life teeming around me, I felt that otherworldly feeling come over me again.

Just like all the other places that I had traveled to, this destination was in such contrast to my daily surroundings that I found myself captivated and amazed. Blueheads and parrotfish darted around everywhere as I looked on, amazed. It was a familiar feeling, one that I was growing to love, this sensation that I was on a different planet entirely. It wasn't long before a sea ray glided its way over the corals toward me. It felt ethereal; it moved effortlessly as it passed by. It was a perfect start to the day.

We got back to Key Largo a little before lunchtime. I sat on the dock and pulled out my phone to check my reservations farther south. The rest of the passengers headed off the dock, thanking Patrice for his time and expertise. He wished them well and then turned to see me, still trying to get a signal.

"Yuh lost or something, Mistah? Boat ride be done for today."

"Oh no, I'm sorry, just checking on my reservations," I replied.

"Where yuh headed after dis?" he asked.

"Well, I guess it's not really where, but *what* is next." I removed Charlie's list from my shoulder bag and flipped to the page about the Keys. "So, my friend planned this list of things for us to do and see down here. I don't really have a firm itinerary; I just need to fit everything in."

Patrice studied the list quickly, nodding his head. "Yuh friend, why he not wid yuh?"

My shoulders dipped a little. "Ah, well, he passed away about a year ago." Honestly, I was getting tired of having to retell the story each time I met someone new. It felt like scratching a scar; it didn't hurt as much as it used to, but it was still a reminder of the pain. So, I stopped short to see what kind of questions Patrice might have. To my relief, he didn't pry.

"I see," was his reply. "So yuh come down here all alone to honor yuh bruddah? I respect dat."

There was a solemn understanding in his eyes that made me pause and study his expression for a second. He had a weathered kindness about him. It reminded me of something Myles said once—that kind people seldom had easy lives. My curiosity got the better of me. "You say that like someone who's been through it?"

He nodded slowly, looking up into the sky. "I come here, much like yuh, to honor someone. But my story be a bit different."

I put my phone back in my shoulder bag. "Well, I've got six more days to do what will probably only take me three. So, time is on my side for once. Feel like sharing that story over lunch?"

I had no idea where this sudden burst of extroversion came from. It seemed very out of character for me, but for once I wasn't afraid of his response.

Well, that's new, I thought to myself.

Patrice looked back at me, confused. "What yuh say again?"

"Sure, its lunchtime, right? I mean, unless you've got other tours. I don't want to keep you if you have other obligations," I said, trying to be accommodating.

"Ha! I like yuh, mainlander. No, I don't got no obligations except to Patrice Thompson. Made sure of dat long ago."

He looked at me and scratched the side of his head. "Yuh different from da other tourists. Tell yuh what, tree blocks down on da left be a food truck run by a lovely lady—name's Jade. She make da best seafood tacos in Key Largo. Yuh go dere. I gonna clean up da boat and mi soon come."

I looked down the road where he was pointing and nodded my head. "Three blocks on the left, seafood tacos. See you soon."

Sure enough, right where he had suggested, there was a little food truck called Conchy Jade's, and the loud, boisterous lady in the window must have been Jade. I ordered my food and found a place to sit. A few minutes after that, Patrice appeared, and the shop owner waved and shouted at him. He walked over to her, and they embraced through the window. She had a glow in her eyes as they talked. She started to fix him something in the back of the truck as they continued to converse. He made her laugh several times. Patrice had a ton of charisma. He was a natural conversationalist. He noticed me with an acknowledging head bob while he was waiting for his food. Once it was ready, he grabbed a seat across from me.

"Have you always been that smooth, or did somebody teach you?" I joked, complimenting him.

He let out a short laugh. "Do yuh know Ralph Waldo Emerson?"

"The poet? Yeah, I've heard of him," I said, nodding my head.

"Well, I'll use da man's words— 'No one will ever know da violence it took to become dis gentle.'"

I raised a curious eyebrow. "Try me."

Patrice and I chatted for almost three hours. I shared a more complete version of my story, including life in New York, my travels so far, and the events that brought me to the Keys. He shared a lot about his upbringing. More than I expected. His story unfolded like the slow illumination of lanterns on some unseen path. It held my attention like a trance.

Patrice and his older brother Delroy were foster kids for as long as he could remember. They never knew their birth parents and bounced around from one foster family to another. Mostly, though, they lived on the streets of West Kingston in Jamaica.

He shared with me that the only place he and Delroy really felt any kind of family connection was with other street kids, and so naturally they fell in with the local gangs. Unfortunately, that also meant that they got wrapped up in a lot of violent crime.

He talked at length about the hard times they went through—fights, drugs, weapons deals, brushes with death. Patrice saw the control that the gangs had over his brother and knew they'd both end up dead if they stayed in that world. He confronted Delroy, saying that they could just move north, find jobs in Negril or Montego, and start over. However, his brother flatly refused, telling him that his place was in Kingston.

So, Patrice began to distance himself as best he could, finding odd jobs as a dockworker at the Freeport Terminal. After a while, he scraped together enough money to leave on his own, and at nineteen he moved away. He and Delroy haven't seen or spoken to each other since.

"I try hard, real hard, to make him change his weys, but soon his whole life one big mess. He followed all da wrong people. Everything go bad-bad for him. We stopped talking when I moved. Bettah dat wey. Sometime yuh gotta cut one to save another."

His words were methodical and deliberate; he dressed up old pain in quiet humor, his life a rugged sail of hope he had slowly stitched together. His experiences were vast, unimaginable, but achingly human. I found myself holding my breath as he continued, almost afraid that if I spoke up it would shatter the spell and he would stop.

"Mi bruddah, he heard da words I was speakin' in his ears, but his heart kept none of dem. So, I left mi home on a bus to Montego. I found work at da resorts for a few years. Bounced around doing da same work in da Caymans and Bahamas until I became a citizen of da Keys."

It was like he had prepared this story for years, molding vivid memories into rich metaphors, waiting for the right person to tell. It felt less like I was listening to him and more like I was witnessing his life.

"Mainlanders love spending money down here, and I was happy to help dem. But, I nevah forgot Delroy. I swore dat would not be mi fate. So, I decide to honor mi lost bruddah by working only for Patrice. Now I own a few businesses, I got a vacation rental in Key West I live in half da year, and I make enough money to own mi life."

He leaned back in his chair and laced his fingers behind his head. I could tell he was proud of his accomplishments. I was impressed. He had two things I craved—confidence and independence.

"Imagine that!" I said with a big smile. "Patrice Thompson, street kid from West Kingston turned Florida Keys entrepreneur. What a cool story. Thank you for sharing it."

"Yuh story ain't too shabby neither, Inertia Hollins," he said in reply. "Young Wall Street shut-in turned jet settah, on an adventure in memory of his best friend. Yuh leave da big city for good reason. Many be here just to relax. Yuh come wid purpose."

He nodded slowly. "So yuh decide where to next?"

Checking my phone, I said, "Well, I know I'm headed south until I get to Key West. It'd be cool to see sights along the way. Mangroves and paddleboarding are definite, and I've got to have a slice of key lime pie while I'm here. The rest is flexible."

Patrice folded his arms and tilted his head to the side a little. It seemed like he was considering something deeply. He looked at me intensely, almost like he was sizing me up.

"I gonna take a chance on yuh, Inertia. I was headed south too. I gotta check on mi rental property and meet some friends. I know da best places to see da mangroves, and I got paddleboards to use as well. If yuh interested, I will join yuh, introduce yuh to mi friends, and in return yuh get da real Salt Life experience." Then he reached out his hand for me to shake.

I looked down at his outstretched hand. "A travel buddy?!" I said excitedly. "How could I turn you down?!"

I reached across the table, and we shook on it. Genuinely, I was glad to have him along. We had only met that day, but our conversation was deep and real, and I really didn't like traveling alone. Life is better with people; the lesson resurfaced again.

Also, having a local along meant that I would see all the best places and avoid the major tourist traps. After lunch, we walked back to the dock, and Patrice went to put the covers on his boat while I pulled the car around to pick him up. He walked up to my rental car with a small duffle bag in his hand, shaking his head.

"We going to Key West in this?! I not gonna fit, no chance."

It wasn't that small of a car, but Patrice was a tall guy. His apprehension was understandable, but I was sure he'd be fine. I decided to risk a bit of his own native dialect to encourage him.

"Patrice, yuh gonna be irie," I said with a big smile.

He let out a big laugh and said, "Oh yuhs from de islands now?! No sah! Listen to Mistah Big City speaking Patois to get Patrice inna his tiny Cooper!

"Just have a little faith, Patrice. No worries, right?" I said, trying to convince him.

Continuing to shake his head, he tossed his bag in back and attempted to sit in the passenger seat. As I expected, and much to his own surprise, he fit easily. We had a good laugh about it and set off south. He pointed out a few places to stop along the way. I rushed about taking pictures, and Patrice again reminded me to slow down.

"Yuh movin' too fast, Inertia. Yuh grabbin' up dem seconds like dey owe yuh money! Life is a gift, bruddah. Savor it. Don't be trappin' every instant on yuh phone."

He's right. I need to slow down, I thought.

The trip south was a joy. We grabbed dinner at this cool little place with a literal thatched roof that had more of the amazing seafood that the area was known for. He knew the owners, of course, and they treated us like royalty. We sat behind huge piles of shells and scraps from our meal as they kept bringing us out new things to try. There was a live band playing, and we chatted late into the night with the owners as the sounds of laughter and steel drums filled the air.

Before we parted ways for the evening, he told me where to meet him in the morning to go paddleboarding. Patrice and I shook hands again, and he dapped me up like an old friend. I took it as a high honor. I remember it feeling like another turning point. I was someplace new with someone new, we had become friends, and we made plans to meet up in the morning to do something I had never done before. The old Inertia would never have taken these chances. He would have played it safe and made himself smaller, and in the process sacrificed his own joy. What a difference a few trips had made. Travel really was good medicine.

"Inna di morrows, Inertia Hollins," Patrice said as he walked away.

"Have a good night, Patrice. Thanks for taking a chance on me."

șɵșɵ

The next morning started better than I could have hoped. Patrice met me at the designated spot with a big smile and two cups in his hand. He handed one of them to me.

"Wah gwaan, Big City. Yuh drink coffee?"

I laughed at the nickname. "I'm from Manhattan, Patrice. What do you think?"

"I had a feeling. Here, a special treat for yuh. Cuban coffee, it be lightnin' in a cup. Enjoy."

It smelled amazing. I took a small sip. It was the perfect drinking temperature, and holy cow was it strong! Too much of that stuff, and I might never have slept again!

We walked to the shore, where we met some of his friends and their children. I got a quick lesson on paddleboarding. It was a lot like a kayak, except the oar was longer, and you were standing. After we finished our coffee, we launched off the shore and made our way out to these dense areas of mangroves that were more like a forest on water than the little patches of trees I had expected. The water below us was super clear, only about ten feet deep, and you could see all the ocean life below us.

Patrice knew the mangrove patches like the back of his hand and led us through all these twisting, meandering waterways through dense areas around the shoreline. It was so thick in some areas we had to lie down on our paddleboards and propel ourselves with our hands to duck under the reaching branches. Tiny little sea crabs skittered overhead on the branches, and thousands (not exaggerating) of fish flashed by in streaks of silver and blue as they rushed under our paddleboards in large schools. After about an hour, we stopped on a small sandbar and had lunch. While the kids searched for shells and critters, Patrice asked me about Charlie.

"So, it been a year since yuh friend pass? Have yuh made peace wid it yet?"

"I think so. I used to carry around a lot of guilt about it. Not anymore. I still grieve from time to time. It's a weird thing, grief. I'm not sure it will ever go away. It shows up unannounced and grabs ahold of me. It happens randomly. Sometimes I just feel sad. Know what I mean?"

He nodded appreciatively. "Ya, sure-sure. Let me tell yuh bruddah, death be a part of life. It come for everyone. Saw plenty of it back home. We all gonna owe da Ferryman his coins someday. But before he take us to dat next place, we gotta learn to love dis one. Dat grief yuh feel is not bad. It be all da love we nevah got to share. Appreciate dat grief. It make yuh strong but not cold. Grief be proof of joy."

And just like that, it happened again, like the universe had put all these people in my path to teach me life's great lessons.

"That's a great perspective, Patrice. How'd you become so wise?" I asked.

"Da pace of da Keys give yuh time to think. Can't see yuh reflection in da waves, to see dat, to see yuh real self, yuh must wait for calm waters," he said, looking off into the distance.

Then he turned to me again, "So what's left on yuh list, Big City?"

"Well, the southernmost point looks interesting but also a little overrated. I'm not standing in line for a selfie next to an oversized buoy. Really, the only thing left on my list is to find a good slice of key lime pie."

"Pie? Well, bruddah, da best place for key lime pie gotta be da Moondog. It's a café next to da Hemmingway Home. I take yuh there tonight."

We paddled back to the shore, and we were fortunate enough to catch sight of a small pod of dolphins that were making their way out to sea. We said our goodbyes to Patrice's friends and biked through the neighborhoods to the café for dinner. I had a great sandwich and a tall glass of iced tea. Then, as promised, we both got a slice of their famous key lime pie. It comes with a thick layer of toasted meringue, and it totally lived up to the hype. Sweet, tart, and smooth as silk; it was everything a pie lover could ask for.

"I found it, Charlie," I said as I finished my last forkful. Patrice smiled. I was sure that, somewhere, Charlie was smiling too.

Over the next several days, Patrice introduced me to many of his friends—shop owners, chefs, musicians. The people of Key West are a wonderful bunch. They call themselves Conchs, and for a hot minute, they declared their independence from the mainland. "Conch Republic" signs dot the landscape down there. They're very proud of their heritage and culture. It was refreshing to be immersed in a lifestyle that wasn't skyscrapers, commuter traffic, and crowds. Charlie used to say that it was easy to get wrapped up in the unhappy urgency of our times. Not in the Keys. Things are much slower. Island time is a real thing, and it's wonderful. It made perfect sense why this destination was on his list.

At the end of the week, the ride back to the mainland was slow and full of emotion. I didn't want to leave. I promised Patrice I would come back and see him. When I dropped him back off at his boat in Key Largo, he hugged me like family.

"Don't be a stranger, Big City! Walk gud and tek care. Next time yuh in da Keys, bring yuh friends. We show dem what dat Salt Life be like."

"I will, Patrice. Thank you for everything."

"Bless up yuhself, bruddah!" he said as I pulled away.

Later that day, right before I boarded my flight, I opened my journal and added, *Patrice Thompson, Key West—"Grief is all the love we never got to share. Grief is proof of joy."*

I pressed my head against the seat and got comfortable as the crew began the pre-flight safety instructions. Letting my mind drift, I thought back on the amazing week of experiences, the friendship I had formed, and how different it was from the life I typically lived. There were only two locations left on Charlie's list, and the changes in me were extraordinary. When I got back home, it was time to make some other changes as well.

CHAPTER TWELVE

Roof of the World

The plane from Miami had barely touched down, and I was on the phone to my boss.

"Louis?"

"Hollins? It's Sunday. What's wrong?" he replied, confused. "Is your flight delayed?"

"No, we just landed at LaGuardia. But listen. I can't do it anymore, Louis," I said.

"What do you mean, you can't do it anymore?"

"I'm burnt-out. I don't have the stomach for it."

"Hollins, you aren't making any sense. Burnt-out? You just came back from a week in paradise! Don't have the stomach for what!?" he replied, even more confused.

"I can't live my life like this anymore, Louis. I quit."

"Whoa, whoa, take it easy kid. That's a pretty dramatic change. Make sure you know what you're saying. That's not a word you throw around lightly."

There was silence on the line, deliberate and full of anticipation, as I considered what he said.

"I mean it. I'm done."

After my time in the Keys, everything was different. All desire for the frantic pace of the financial markets was gone. I wanted out. Louis exhaled heavily as he composed himself. The tone of his voice smoothed out into the measured, level-headed guy that originally hired me.

"I understand, Inertia"—I knew he was serious because he almost never used my first name— "However, you're one of my best traders, and you know I *really hate* losing talent. Come in tomorrow and let's talk. If, after we've talked, you're still set on leaving, I won't stop you. Fair?"

"Yeah, that's fair, Louis."

"Good," he replied. "I'll see you in the morning."

He hung up. I hustled across the jet bridge into the crowd of busy travelers, replaying the conversation in my head. I did feel a bit of loyalty to the guy. He was incredibly reasonable and compassionate when Charlie died, so there was a sense of obligation to at least hear his idea.

Sitting at the breakfast bar of my apartment the next morning before leaving for work, I looked down at Charlie's list. The next destination wasn't just far away; it was in a different country.

"Visit Iceland," I said aloud to myself.

The potential stops for this destination filled the next three pages, and I knew I couldn't do them all. I didn't have the budget or the vacation days to spare.

Sorry, old friend, I am going to have to make some choices on this one.

As I rode the elevator up to the office, I started to work out the logistics of the next several months. My plan was to live off my savings and the balance of Charlie's "adventure account" until I figured out my next move. At the very least, I knew I'd be able to finish his list of destinations.

The elevator doors parted to that familiar bronze lion, my silent buddy Leonidas, ever present. I rubbed the top of his head.

When I entered Louis's office, he stood to greet me with a firm handshake. Unsure of what to expect, I sat down in one of the chairs that faced his desk.

He looked at me and said very plainly, "I can't lose you, Hollins. At least, not for another six months or so. There are junior associates that show a lot of potential, but I need more time."

"What's your plan?" I asked, half-heartedly, convinced there was nothing he could offer me to keep me around.

He suggested that I shift away from day trading and start working on things that were easier to manage, like mutual funds. I'd lose my bonus, but it was a good midpoint between salary and workload. It would mean fewer hours but a living income. It would also allow me to maintain a bit of that carefree life I had enjoyed with Patrice. It was a perfect fit.

⇽⇾⇽⇾

My research on Iceland was *extensive*. I needed to pare down Charlie's list by almost two-thirds to fit it into a reasonable vacation schedule. It looked like July was my best window to see the things that really stirred my heart. I found a company with these cool little campervans for rent. You could travel on your own, or they also had a guided trip where you caravanned with a local. After my experience with Patrice in the Keys, local knowledge seemed like a great idea.

Once the flight landed and I grabbed my bags, I made my way over to the reservation desk to pick up my rolling home for the next ten days. It was then that something remarkable happened. When I got to the reservation desk, a familiar voice filled my ears. A young woman with fair skin and raven hair that fell to about her shoulders was ahead of me, speaking with the agent. I stopped dead in my tracks.

It couldn't be.

The rep that was helping her handed back her passport and said, "Thank you for your identification, Ms. Royce. It'll only be a few minutes."

"Violet!?"

The woman immediately stiffened, then turned quickly to face me. Those intense aquamarine eyes locked with mine, and her face lit up with excitement and surprise.

"Oh my God!! Inertia!?! What are you doing here?!"

I was dumbfounded at the sight of her. My breath forgot its rhythm, my eyes grew wide, and everything seemed to fall away except her.

"I could ask you the same thing!" I replied in shock.

"Holy cow, this is crazy! Like, completely insane! How are you?!"

She reached out her arms and gave me a quick, polite hug. I could feel myself blushing immediately. We stepped out of the reservation line for a second to catch up. Like she said when we first met, she loved to travel, and this was her next trip.

"I needed to get out of the city," she said. "Not only was I overdue another adventure, but I needed to get some distance from my ex."

"Your ex?"

"Ugh, sadly. Yeah, it's kind of a tragic story. Do you remember that day in the coffee shop?"

I rolled my eyes. "How could I forget?"

A mischievous grin came across her face. "Your next words better not be an apology."

They were going to be, I thought.

She continued. "Anyway, the guy that ghosted me right before we met? Yeah, so, he said he had a legitimate emergency, and I gave him a second chance. Ugh, what a mistake."

I listened intently, unsure of what she'd say next.

She sighed heavily. "We got in this huge fight. During the argument, some stuff came up that didn't make sense. Messages and absences that didn't add up. I questioned him about them, and he just got angrier. He twisted my words and ..."

She stopped short and shook her head, exasperated, almost like she was trying to shake off a bad dream. "Whatever. He's a liar. I ended the relationship about ten days ago. I booked the first flight I could find."

It felt like there was more to the story than what she was sharing. "Sounds like that was hard," I offered.

She shrugged. "Yeah. The trouble was, things were really good for a little while, but I could never really tell with him."

"Tell what?"

She stuck her hands in her coat pockets and looked up at the ceiling. "I could never tell if he was a good person that made a lot of poor choices, or if he was a bad person that did enough good to cover it up."

It was a profound statement. Reflecting on it, I think we've all had a few people in our lives that wronged us with some consistency and then made a habit of trying to apologize after.

"What did you decide?" I asked cautiously.

"The latter," she said remorsefully.

Just then, someone behind us dropped a bag that made a loud noise. We both looked to see what had happened. When Violet turned, it side-swept the hair that covered the left side of her face. I noticed a mostly healed bruise over the top corner of her left eye. She turned back quickly, realizing what had happened.

"Violet, did he ...?" I stopped, not wanting to finish the question.

She nodded, staring at the floor.

"I was an idiot. I thought he might change, and when he didn't, I don't know why I was afraid to leave him," she replied.

I didn't know what to say. I was flooded with a mix of emotions—anger, despair, regret. I couldn't imagine how she must have felt.

"That's awful. I'm so sorry, Violet."

"Don't be." She moved the hair away from her face, exposing the bruise again and tilting it toward me. "I left him the night this happened, and I lawyered up the next morning. He's gonna regret it."

I was impressed by her resilience. Most people, me included, would have been buried under a mountain of self-worth issues or wrapped up in a cycle of apologies and recurrences. Violet was a rare person. It must have been terrible, but she seemed stronger for it.

"Anyway, I don't know why I'm spilling my guts to you again, but I'm sick of talking about my ex," she said, pushing my shoulder. "What the heck are you doing way out here? Iceland is a long way from Lucian's café in Nolita."

She stopped and took a short step back. "Wait, have you been following me?"

I shook my head, embarrassed. "Oh my God, no, I promise! In fact, I was convinced I'd never see you again after I made a such a fool of myself at the café."

She relaxed. A grin crept across her face.

"You did fumble pretty hard that day," she said with a laugh. "Like, epically. God, running back into you is unbelievable! We were probably on the same plane! How did I not see you?!"

I shrugged. "I was thinking the same thing! We couldn't have been more than twenty feet apart the whole flight. Seeing you again is surreal."

She shifted a little and took a step closer to me.

"It really is. Inertia, can I share something with you? I mean, that sounds ridiculous considering how I blabbed on about my ex."

I nodded. "Of course. And you don't sound ridiculous. People have a habit of oversharing around me—happens a lot."

She smiled. "I bet it does."

And there it was again. That pull. That unseen attraction. There was something about that moment. I'll remember it forever. It felt like this crazy coincidence had become something more. Call it a spark, or fate, or chemistry—it was undeniable.

"Anyway, I only have a few regrets in my life, Inertia. One of them is dating the prick that gave me this bruise." She fiddled with her luggage tag, hesitating. "Another was not walking back into that café to hand you my number anyway."

My heart rate practically doubled right on the spot.

"Really?" I asked, surprised.

"Really."

She reached into her purse and pulled out a pen. Grabbing my wrist, she began writing her number on my hand.

"But I thought you didn't believe in that fate crap," I replied.

"I don't. But I'm not wasting a second chance either. Especially one like this. Like, what are the odds? One in a million?"

Probably more than that, I thought.

I looked down at my hand and immediately pulled out my phone, entering the number in. I sent a text with a smiley face. Seconds later, her purse chimed as the text came through. She giggled.

"There's something about you, Inertia. I'm not sure what it is, but I feel like I need to hear your story, especially what brought you to Iceland at the same time as me."

The accident flashed through my mind quickly, like a splinter in my brain, followed by a flood of all the events after it that led up to this moment.

"Oh God, that could take a while. How much time you got?" I asked.

She bit her lower lip as she looked down at her reservation ticket and then back up at me. "About a week and a half."

My breath quickened a little. "Wait, what do you mean?"

She smiled. "Well, we were in the same line. That means you probably had the same idea I did, right? Rent a van to see the sights?"

"Yeah, I did actually ..."

"That's what I thought. OK, now here's the million-dollar question—are you going it alone, or did you opt for the guided trip?"

I couldn't believe this was happening. It felt like a dream.

"I chose the guide."

Her smile grew even bigger. "Me too."

"So that means ..."

The realization was like a tide of wildfire—brilliant, reckless, and uncontained. She removed a white knit hat from her coat pocket. Pulling it over her hair, she looked up at me, her eyes alive with possibility.

"So, that means we've got plenty of time for you to tell me everything."

⌘⌘⌘

Our guide for the expedition was a soft-spoken man with short, unkempt blonde hair and a friendly disposition named Fridrik. He had lived in Iceland his whole life. I was convinced his ancestors must have been Vikings because he was a tall, broad-shouldered mountain of a man. However, like most big guys that I've encountered, he was a total teddy bear once you got to know him better.

He started his adult life as a fisherman on his father's boat until he saved enough money to buy a few campervans and start his own business giving tours around the country. I admired his entrepreneurialism and his zest for life. He reminded me a lot of Patrice.

Fridrik had his own campervan, like Violet and I did, and there were two other vehicles in our group—a middle-aged Norwegian couple making their fifth trip to Iceland and two young guys from Oregon that were first-timers like us. Violet sat on the front bumper of her van as Fridrik went over the general itinerary. I walked next to her, zipping up my coat and putting on a hat. Even though it was late July, most of Iceland was just south of the Arctic Circle, so it was chilly. The weather, in general, was unpredictable. Fridrik told us to dress for all four seasons, rain or shine.

Our trip would take us counterclockwise around the country, with our last few days in Iceland's capital city, Reykjavik (Rayk-yah-veek).

"This is going to be awesome," Violet said.

"Ha, that's funny," I replied.

"What's that?"

"Something my buddy's mom said a while back. She was right. I'm looking forward to the discomfort of unfamiliar things."

She nodded appreciatively. "That's the spirit!"

However, our first unfamiliar thing was very comforting. The famous Blue Lagoon is only a short drive from the airport. I thought it might be a little overrated because it's so heavily promoted, but it turned out to be amazing. The hot, milky blue water sinks deep. It enveloped you like liquid moonlight. We seemed to dissolve into the mist. The clouds felt closer, as it was hard to distinguish between lagoon and sky. It was a perfect way to recharge after the long flight.

Upon leaving the Blue Lagoon, we hit Iceland's ring road that circles the country. You wouldn't believe the views—dark sand, crashing waves, deep shifting clouds above mossy hills. Occasionally, light would break through the clouds and then vanish again, leaving only the rawness of the landscape. I was immediately captivated by the country's natural beauty.

However, I struggled to pronounce any of the locations properly. Thankfully, Fridrik was very patient and coached me on proper Icelandic pronunciations. As we approached our next stop, the cloud cover broke, and long beams of sunlight dotted the landscape. It was then we caught our first glimpse of Seljalandsfoss (sell-ya-lahnds-foss).

This tall waterfall breaks over a high cliff with a walking path that allows you to get behind the water as it plummets to the pool below. Stilled with reverence at the sight, we watched the cascading water catch in the wind, creating a large, misty cloud. With even a gentle breeze, Seljalandsfoss covers the path in a steady spray. It felt like the countryside waving to greet us as we wandered along the path. Despite our rain gear, we still got completely drenched.

Drying off back at the vans before heading to our next spot, Violet asked, "So, that story, the one that might take a while, let's hear it."

"Now?" I asked, towel-drying my hair.

"This is as good a time as any," she replied.

She threw me a bright-yellow, short-range walkie-talkie. She tapped an identical one in her other hand and said, "I'll be on channel seven."

As we traveled further east to our next destination past the mossy landscape and small herds of sheep and rams along the foothills, I shared everything—Charlie's story, his family, his passing, the list, my friends back home, my own internal doubts and struggles, the solo adventures, the people I met—all of it. It was surprisingly therapeutic. The time flew by, and before I knew it, we had arrived at our last stop for the day. As we hopped out of the vans, Violet quickly ran up to me and hugged me.

The sudden affection was unexpected, so I stood there like a surprised statue, arms at my sides as she squeezed me.

"You put a lot of trust in me, sharing all that," she said, wiping her eye. "I even teared up a little. Jerk."

Turning, we looked ahead at one of the most famous and picture-worthy waterfalls in all of Iceland.

"Quite the sight, isn't she!?" Fridrik said with a wide smile as we approached the base of the trail.

The famous Skogafoss cascades over black rock cliffs that take a sheer drop two hundred feet to the pool below. The water roars like a dragon—a thick curtain of fury against the moss-covered cliffs as it crashes to the ground. There is so much spray that even with a hint of sunshine, Skogafoss will consistently produce a rainbow, sometimes two.

We laughed and shouted all the way to the base of the crashing water, overcome by the echoing voice of the falls. Violet grabbed my hand, pulling me toward the spray, stretching her arms wide. Standing at its base, I felt alive and free, like something primal and savage broke loose inside me.

Later that evening, we camped at sites in full view of the waterfall and made dinner, warming ourselves with hot cocoa and blankets. Hearing the steady sound of crashing water in the distance was hypnotic. Despite the time of day, it still wasn't dark because Iceland gets twenty-plus hours of light that time of year. They call it the midnight sun, and it makes sleeping a real challenge if you don't have something to cover your eyes.

Much later that night, Violet and I sat on folding chairs watching the sun skip off the horizon and begin to climb into the sky again. We sat in silence for a while until she looked over at me inquisitively and asked, "If you could see him again, what would you say?"

I assumed she meant Charlie. I thought about it for a minute. Of the millions of things that I wished I could have said or asked, one question rose above them all.

"I'd ask him why he chose me."

Her brow furrowed a little. "Explain. What do you mean?"

"Out of all the people we knew in high school and college that adored him, of all his fans and friends and social contacts in the city, he regarded me as his, and I quote, 'very best friend in the whole world.' I never understood why. It never made any sense. What could I possibly offer a guy like him to be considered his best friend?"

Violet rolled her eyes. "What a stupid question."

Her response took me by surprise. "Huh? How so?"

She glared at me, stunned. "Oh my God, seriously!? You're not messing with me? You don't see it at all?!"

"See what?" I replied, confused.

She shook her head dismissively.

"Inertia, you are a magnet of calm. Seriously, I know you feel insecure, and you said you're stuck in your head too much, but dude, real talk? You're probably the most approachable person I've ever met."

I raised my eyebrows in quiet disbelief. She was undeterred.

"Oh? You disagree? You said it yourself; people overshare with you all the time, right? I bet you constantly find out things about strangers than they would never tell anyone else. You probably get their whole life story after a few minutes of conversation."

I thought of all the people I'd met through Charlie. There were plenty of parties where I spent the whole evening listening to someone share their deepest secrets with me. It *did* happen a lot. I thought about how quickly I became friends with the Margolis's, Alicia and Samm, Auggie and Katrina. Even Patrice was forthcoming with his story and befriended me almost immediately. *She was right.* People were surprisingly comfortable with me unusually fast.

Seeing my contemplative stare, she nodded confidently.

"Yup, I thought so. Inertia, I had never felt more seen in my whole life than that day in the café. Now, consider how that went—you spilled my coffee, then froze up like some kind of psycho, fumbled over your words, and kicked me in the shin!"

I blushed, remembering in extreme clarity. Not my best day.

"Despite all of that, I felt completely at ease talking to you. We chatted for, what, five or ten minutes? I told you about my parents! I almost gave you my number! Who would do that?! You hear how crazy that sounds, right?!"

I nodded, wide-eyed.

"Inertia, meeting you was one of the most honest and disarming moments of my life. I felt better on my way home that rainy Tuesday than I have in *years*."

She threw her hands to her sides. "See! Here I go again, spilling my guts! I bet you could interrogate a spy with a friendly smile! That's your superpower. You're like the eye of a hurricane. You radiate stillness, even if you can't feel it yourself. And if Charlie was the kind of person you say he was, then I think you've got it backward."

She stood and folded her chair up, prepping to turn in for the night. "I think you were his safe harbor, not the other way around."

The comment struck me like the sound of shattering glass; an explosion of realization reverberated against me. I let out a big exhale, realizing I had been holding my breath as she was speaking.

"Violet, I ... I don't know what to say."

"How about goodnight? I'm beat, and the sun is clearly not setting, which is cool but also frustrating, so I'm going to try and get some rest. We've got a lot more Iceland left to see."

⋄⋄⋄⋄

I barely slept at all. How could I? Her words were like discovering fire, turning lead to gold, or finding the city of Atlantis. It turned my whole life on its head. Could it have been possible all these years that *I* was Charlie Margolis's person, instead of the other way around?

I lay there in my van watching the sun paint the sky, replaying nearly every conversation I ever had with anyone. Each memory seemed to prove Violet's point. It had been right in front of my face my whole life, and I'd never noticed it until now. People didn't gravitate to me like Charlie, but once we talked, they opened up like we had been friends for decades.

The next morning (not that I could tell with near constant daylight), we packed quickly and headed to one of the more well-known black sand beaches called Reynisfjara (ray-nis-fyah-rah). After a quick lesson on the dangers of "sneaker waves," Fridrik made us a traditional Icelandic breakfast of buttered dark rye bread and arctic char as we watched the waves break on the beach.

I scooped a little of the black sand into a small pouch as a keepsake. At Reynisfjara, the quiet feels heavy. Thick clouds began to build along the horizon, and the sand stretched out in front of us, contrasting with the sky like a deep, looming shadow. Large hexagonal basalt columns rose up the walls of the cliffs surrounding the beach like geometric step stones. Violet and I walked toward them. It was easy to imagine the days when Viking longships dotted the shoreline.

"I meant what I said last night," Violet said as we approached the wall of dark stone. "Every word of it."

"Thanks, Violet," I replied, still processing the conversation.

"Call me Vee."

"A nickname already?" I asked.

She shrugged with a smile. "Why not? And what should I call you?"

"My friends call me Ersch."

"Nah, I like your full name better."

After a while on the beach, we drove northwest to the town of Vik (veek) for fuel and provisions before heading northwest to the Jokulsarlon (yo-cool-sar-loan) glacier lagoon. I was really looking forward to this stop, and it turned out to be a completely lights-out breathtaking experience. The lagoon is like stepping into a fantasy novel. Massive, towering, odd-shaped ice formations meander slowly across the lagoon toward the ocean. They called to me like sirens. I wanted to climb on them and explore the peaks and caverns on some of the larger icebergs.

The wind was ever present, whispering to the would-be explorer. This was not the Iceland that I saw on social media. This was the raw and relentless version, that made you gaze into the awe-inspiring landscape and yearn to become a part of it.

"Woah. This is bonkers! The pictures of this place don't even come close," Violet said in awe.

Fridrik sat down between us. "They never do. In Icelandic, you would say, *Myndavélin mín nær þessu ekki*—my camera can't capture this."

Another stop on the trip that defied all pictures with its amazing and otherworldly beauty was Studlagil (stuth-lah-geel) canyon, the largest concentration of basalt columns in Iceland. One of the trails goes along the canyon wall at the water's edge like a stairway along the basalt.

Of the places I visited on my travels, nothing compared to the completely foreign landscape of this place. It was like we had wandered into some alien's home world. We were surrounded in a narrow canyon by tall, curving stacks of basalt sectioned into regular rows like they had been placed there by some large creature. Cutting down the middle of the canyon were the deep turquoise waters of the glacial river that runs through it. I was awestruck. Violet bounced down the basalt sections like a child bounding down the stairs on Christmas morning. She would frequently look back and shoot me little grins.

❧ ❧ ❧ ❧

We started the return trip of our journey with the largest and most powerful waterfall the country had to offer. Deep in the heart of Iceland's volcanic wilderness is Dettifoss. At over three hundred feet wide, this relentless silvery torrent thunders like ancient war drums, echoing in the surrounding canyon. The sound is so intense you can feel the ground shaking. Nature does not call here; it challenges.

We walked right up to the water's edge of this behemoth, another deeply humbling experience for me. We spent a long time sitting there listening to the roar of the falls. Violet kept taking pictures of me, like I would disappear if she didn't capture every second. The way she looked at me made my heart race. I had never felt this way about anyone before. Maybe I was influenced by the awe and wonder of our surroundings, but my affection for her seemed to grow by the day. I only hoped the feeling was mutual.

For the next few days, we headed southwest, taking in sections of the Golden Circle roadway on our way to the capital, Reykjavik. The volcanic landscape was incredible. Long, sweeping, mossy prairie would give way to huge shards of rocks in deep piles that formed the enormous craggy hills that surrounded us. Soon enough, the lights and bustle of civilization were in sight.

We spent the last three days walking around the city and sampling the food. On the last full day before the flight home, I spent a little time alone, reliving the trip in my mind. Iceland had permanently altered my brain chemistry. Words like beautiful and awe-inspiring fell totally flat in the description of this place. I made a promise to myself that I would return.

The raw, rugged power of the natural landscape spoke to something deep in my heart like Yellowstone, and the redwoods, and my time in the Keys. The world was wide and wonderful, and each little piece of it that I got to see silently went to work transforming me. These people, these destinations, they were part of who I was now.

"So, what should we do with our last night in Iceland, Fridrik?" Violet asked.

"Funny you should ask. I am headed someplace tonight. Do you listen to electronic dance music?"

"Like the stuff they play in clubs?" I asked.

He nodded. "Something like that."

I looked over at Violet. "First official date?"

She nodded excitedly.

"OK, Fridrik, lead the way."

We drove to a more industrial section of town and parked outside a large warehouse with no windows. Melodic bass filled the air outside the building. As we entered, we were met with streaks of green and blue laser light. The place was packed. Red and white strobe lights briefly illuminated the crowd; there must have been hundreds of people. Violet and I began to squeeze our way through.

The atmosphere was trancelike, moving images flashing on the walls as we moved through the space. We couldn't help but dissolve into the music and just stomp the ground in sync with the massive crush of people surrounding us. The energy of that place was visceral and tribal. Violet held my hands as we danced and cheered along with everyone else.

The two of us had been flirting with each other for most of the trip, and in that dark, crowded Icelandic rave, the anticipation and curiosity became too great to contain. She wrapped her arms around my neck and drew herself up onto her toes. She pulled herself in closer to me, staring into my eyes, her expression sick with longing. The sides of her mouth drew up into the corners of her cheeks in that signature "up-to-something" grin I'd grown to love. Even in the dimly lit space, her eyes cast their deep blue intensity, and I felt like I could lose myself in them forever.

"What should I believe, Violet Royce, your smile or your eyes?" Our foreheads and noses touched softly.

"How about both," she replied, her voice low and breathy as she slowly tilted her head.

Our lips met in a soft kiss, but it felt more like ignition than contact. A current ran over my skin and down my spine. The whole world just stopped. Everything froze, like the universe had paused to watch two stars collide.

I lifted her off the ground, lacing my fingers together against her lower back. She held on, tightly wrapping her legs around my waist. Then, grabbing both sides of my face with her hands, she leaned in, and we kissed again. Immersed in passion, our touch became raw energy, every feeling intensified, every nerve lit up with the ache of lust and surrender.

I stood there wrapped in her embrace for as long as I could before setting her back down to catch my breath.

"Wow ... that was—" she began.

"Yeah, it was," I said before she could finish. "I've been wanting to do that the whole trip."

With a smile, she placed a soft hand against my cheek and asked, "What took you so long?"

CHAPTER THIRTEEN

Celestial Bodies

We came down the escalator at JFK and headed for the baggage claim. I told Violet that she'd have a chance to meet Alicia and Samm because they were my ride. As the pair came into view, their smiles quickly turned into looks of shock and disbelief as they noticed Violet next to me and my arm around her waist.

"There they are!" I said with a big smile, waving to them.

Samm's jaw dropped open, and Alicia punched her in the side. "Do not embarrass him! Close your mouth right now!"

The shocked expressions on their faces forced immediate introductions. "Violet Royce, these are two of my best friends—Samm Kendricks and her wife Alicia D'Archangelis. Ally, Samm—this is Violet."

Alicia smiled at Violet, and the two embraced quickly and exchanged greetings. Samm stood there, nervously waving her hand. "Uh ... hi?" she said awkwardly.

Violet looked over her shoulder at the baggage claim. "Well, I have my own ride to catch, but Inertia told me a lot about you both, and I'm looking forward to spending more time with you."

She grabbed both lapels of my coat, pulled me in close for a kiss, and said, "And I'll see you much sooner." As she headed for the door, she turned back and waved to the three of us.

Alicia folded her arms with a wry smile. "So, your trip went well?"

On the ride back to my apartment, I told the two of them about the amazing adventure I had in Iceland but refused to answer any questions about Violet. About an hour after I got back to my apartment, Samm FaceTimed me.

"Ersch, it's killing me! I'm seriously freaking out! Please tell me you did not fall in love with some Icelandic oligarch's daughter!?"

"Oh my God, Samm, she lives in Chelsea. Relax."

"She's from New York?!"

"Yes!" I replied, rolling my eyes.

"Did she lose a bet!? Do you owe her money!? What's a total smoke show like that doing with a guy like you?"

I scowled at Samm's image on the screen. "Watch it, Kendricks."

She grinned. "Easy there, science class. I'm just teasing you. Ally says the four of us need to grab dinner ASAP so we can, *ahem*, *get to know her better.*"

She said that last part with air quotes.

"And by *'get to know her better,'* you mean grill her with questions all night like a pair of over-protective aunts?"

Alicia grabbed the phone from Samm, her face appearing on the screen. "Inertia Hollins, how dare you!" She smiled sarcastically. "Neither of us are old enough to be your aunt! We just want to make sure this new lady of yours is a good fit."

Samm's voice came from behind Alicia. "And she's super hot!"

Alicia tilted her head and raised her eyebrows. "Well, that too."

I shook my head at the phone. "You both need to promise you aren't going to scare her off. I really like her. I'm serious."

Samm grabbed the phone back, holding her pinky finger in the air. "Pinky swear, Ersch. We'll be on our best behavior."

"That's what I'm worried about," I replied.

Samm's pursed her lips and held her pinky even closer to the phone.

"Fine," I stammered. "I'll figure out when she's free."

Samm fist-pumped the air. "Nice! We'll set something up for next week. We gotta run to practice—our new show starts in a month, and we've barely got our choreography done." She waved and then handed the phone to Alicia, who blew a kiss at the screen and ended the call.

❧❧❧❧

Alicia booked someplace fancy, of course. I arrived early, hoping it would help settle my nerves. It didn't. In fact, it made it worse. I was so worked up over a simple dinner with Violet and my friends. I remember hyper-fixating on the need for everything to go smoothly. It felt like there was a lot at stake. After Charlie passed, Alicia and Samm were arguably the closest friends I had, and they were meeting the woman I was falling in love with. Suppose they had nothing in common, or worse, ended up hating each other? My mind swam with all these awful scenarios, which just compounded my nervousness.

I fidgeted with my tie and kept checking my phone, waiting for them to arrive. A text came in from Violet, and I looked up to see her approaching from the far side of the dining room. She wore a long, black dress and had her hair up in a tight ball of styled curls. One ringlet of her hair fell to the left side of her face. She looked amazing.

"Awe! Inertia! You look so good in a suit! What a sharp-dressed man you are," Violet said.

I stood to help seat her and push in her chair. "Well, right back at'cha, Vee. You look incredible. You turned every head in the restaurant when you walked in."

"What a gentleman," she replied.

We ordered drinks, and shortly after, Samm and Alicia arrived. Both were dressed very elegantly, like at my birthday dinner. We greeted one another and sat down. I looked at Samm with a smile and said, "I don't know, Kendricks, I think you're starting to like dressing up."

Samm's brow furrowed. "I will knock you out, science class."

I laughed anxiously. "Vee, you'll have to excuse Samm, she's more of a t-shirt and jeans person, if you know what I mean."

"So, basically, my spirit animal," Violet replied. "I always prioritize comfort over fashion. I own one nice dress, and I'm wearing it."

Samm glared at me, nodding in approval. I could feel myself starting to sweat, and I thought that maybe it would be better if I just let the three of them talk. We ordered appetizers, and Violet asked Alicia about their careers in the performing arts.

Alicia grinned. "Well, since I was a little girl, my family was involved in some type of performance entertainment. My father taught theater arts at NYU, and my mother went to Juilliard. Between the two of them, they produced or acted in almost every play I can think of. They met in the industry, and their daughter grew up in the industry, so it's no surprise I gravitated to this life.

When I eventually stumbled upon aerial performing arts, I fell in love. The emotion and spectacle of the circus and the athletic ability of the performers, well, it just set my heart on fire." She shot a quick glance at Samm, squeezing her hand. "Speaking of fire, that's where I met this little fireball and fell in love a second time."

Samm rolled her eyes. "Ugh, you're so corny."

Turning back to Violet, Alicia sipped her wine and said, "So, tell us about yourself, Violet. Is New York home, or are you from elsewhere?"

"No, New York is home. My parents were from Queens," Violet replied. "But before I bore you with stuff you already know, how much has Inertia shared?"

Alicia folded her arms and threw me an irritated frown. "Barely a word, actually."

Violet laughed. "Ha! Well, back to it, I guess. Like I said, I was born and raised in Queens. My parents had me later in life, so I was an only child. Unfortunately, I lost them both to different types of cancer in my early twenties."

"Oh no! God, in your twenties?! That's awful. I'm so sorry," Samm replied.

"Thank you, Samm. It was really hard. They died about eleven months apart. I was barely out on my own, and then I had to put my life on hold to care for them, one right after the other. I became super independent in the process. After they passed, I found a studio apartment in Chelsea near some college friends, which helped add some normalcy back into my life. When the money from my parents' estate ran out, I got a job in the marketing and advertising industry. Turns out I have some natural talent for logo design and branding work."

"Interesting," Alicia said, sipping her wine. "We should connect you with the promotional people for our troupe."

"I would love that," Violet replied. "Currently, I work for a mid-size company near the East Village run by a wonderful couple, Rudy and Georgetta Hill. They treat me like their own daughter. I've been with them for about five years, and I do some freelance work on the side as well. As for when I'm not working, I'm obsessed with travel. I try to go a few places every year. The Hills are very generous with my vacation time, and I'm grateful for that."

So far so good, I thought as Violet continued her story.

"It's a big world, and I hope to see as much of it as I can. In fact, that's how I ran back into this guy," she said, rubbing my arm. "We were both in line for campervans at the Keflavik airport."

"Wait," Samm said, setting her glass down. "*Ran back into him*? I thought you guys met in Iceland?"

Violet giggled. "Well, not exactly."

Sensing a juicy story, Alicia and Samm leaned in closer.

"Go on," Alicia said.

I groaned, knowing what was coming. "Please don't."

"Inertia Hollins, I love the story of how we met," Violet replied.

"Ugh, I was afraid you'd say that."

Our food arrived, and Violet recounted the deeply embarrassing story of our first meeting at Lucian's coffee shop. I felt like she was unnecessarily descriptive, but Alicia and Samm demanded that she give every detail. I picked at my food, feeling my face flush the entire time as the three of them laughed like grade-schoolers, mostly at my expense.

"So, what brings you out today?! That was your line?!" Samm said, eyes wide. "And then you kicked her?! Way to go, Ersch! You're lucky Charlie isn't around to hear this. He would have put you on his podcast. The whole city would have found out how bad you crashed and burned!"

I shoveled another forkful of food in my mouth and shook my head.

She's probably right, I thought.

This wasn't exactly what I'd hoped for this evening, but at least the three of them were enjoying each other's company. By the time dessert was served, they were exchanging numbers and taking selfies together. They got along great. I should have known. I had dreamed up all these terrible outcomes, and none of them ever came to pass. Another good lesson, hidden in the events of my life. Just like most of the things I worried about, my fear was a mile high and a mile wide but paper thin.

I was figuring out the tip for the server when Samm looked at me and said, "See, that wasn't so bad, was it, Ersch? I hope you weren't too nervous."

"Nervous?! Of course I was nervous! It's very important that my closest friends and my girlfriend get along," I replied.

Violet looked at me and raised both eyebrows. *"Girlfriend?* Is that what I am, your *girlfriend?"*

The way she emphasized the word sent me into a mild panic. Should I have asked what we should refer to each other as? Had I assumed too much? Did I just mess up?

I stammered, "I, uh, well, I mean ..."

Violet placed a comforting hand on my knee. "It's OK, Inertia Hollins. I'll be your girlfriend."

Alicia grinned broadly as she sipped her wine. "Oh, Inertia. I like this one."

⚜ ⚜ ⚜

Later that evening, back at my apartment, I picked up Charlie's list. The last destination stared back up at me.

I read it aloud to the empty space. "Visit Zion National Park. Hike Angel's Landing. Spend an evening under the desert sky."

I googled Angel's Landing. The hair on the back of my neck stood straight up, and I immediately broke into a cold sweat.

Of course he'd save this place for last.

Violet was adamant that I was not going to see the southwest without her. So, after about a month of planning, we booked flights and took a long weekend for the final journey in what had been a truly life-changing series of trips.

We landed in Las Vegas at nighttime, which was a cool experience. The city looks like a giant carnival from the air.

The drive the next morning was spectacular. We decided to take the Zion Canyon Scenic Drive. It added about an hour to the trip, but it was well worth it. About a hundred miles outside of Vegas, we passed through the Virgin River Gorge, and every single turn opened up to a view that completely took our breath away. The landscape feels like it was carved by titans. The highway is just a tiny little line weaving through a giant stone cathedral. Massive towers of rock, jagged and sunburnt, jut into the air like the bones of the earth. Everywhere, the landscape is dominated by rust reds, deep terra-cotta ochres, and flashes of green where desert plants cling to the rocks.

We could see the striped rock layers from millions of years ago as we cruised down the winding paths to our destination.

Giant buttes and plateaus tilt this way and that where the land collided and mountains formed.

Zion National Park is primarily the Zion Canyon. It stretches about fifteen miles and is almost three thousand feet deep in some sections. The walls of the canyon rose like ancient sentinels as we approached our accommodations for the night—a sprawling wood and stone lodge with a huge green roof. The Angel's Landing hike requires a permit to make the ascent. Luckily, Violet got us into the seasonal lottery early enough, and we were awarded two permits for the next day.

We started the hike the following morning, well before dawn. About a half mile in, the elevation starts to climb. Angel's Landing rises over fifteen hundred feet to the summit. I wasn't terribly fond of heights but committed to the experience despite my anxiety about the climb. A little before the first mile, the switchbacks started. We gained about three hundred feet of elevation fast. It was a very demanding hike.

After a bit, the trail made a hard left and continued to climb at a much more manageable angle. I was relieved that the path had settled for the moment, but it seemed like as soon as I caught my breath, we hit more switchbacks.

Everywhere we looked felt like a postcard. The sun-warmed cliffs of Navajo sandstone towered above us, etched with time, layered like the pages of some geological fairy tale, each band of rust and amber colored rock reminded me of the rings of the redwood trees and the deafening amplitude of time. We scanned the sides of the cliffs in wonder. It made me feel unbelievably small and the earth impossibly vast, but at the same time, I felt intimately close to it all.

About two miles in, we got our first look at what's referred to as the "chain section." Of all the sketchy things I have done in my life—including getting lost in rough parts of New York

City, trying weird food with my friends, stealing that steamroller in college, and all the various other stupid stuff that I had done throughout the years—hiking the chain section of Angel's Landing was perhaps the sketchiest.

At this point in the hike, the trail is uncomfortably narrow. It's treacherous enough that someone had the foresight to pound a chain railing into the path. We had to walk across the spine of a huge cliff edge. Falling off was probably not survivable. We were way too high up the canyon wall. Violet moved along at an even pace and reached the end of the narrow section with ease. I was incredibly nervous about this part of the trail, and about halfway across, I completely froze.

My voice trembled as I called out to her, "Vee, if I go any further, I'm going to die!"

She shot me a look of annoyance. "You aren't going to die, you big baby. It's only a little hike."

She said "little hike" like it was an afternoon walk in Central Park. I shouted back, "There's nothing little about this!"

She put her hands on her hips and said, "You'll be fine! Come on! One foot in front of the other. It's not rocket surgery!"

"Really?! The metaphor is rocket science *or* brain surgery," I shouted back.

"Mixing metaphors is supposed to have a comedic effect, Mr. Fun Police."

I shook my head, continuing to struggle. "Vee, I'm serious. I don't think I can make it."

"Yes, you can," she replied.

"No, I'm serious!"

Violet let out a long, exasperated sigh. "Oh my God, just get over yourself already!"

"What do you mean?!" I yelled back, unable to take another step.

"You're getting all twisted up in the claws of your own self-doubt again. Put your big-boy pants on and *get over here!*"

I could tell by the tone of her voice that if I didn't get moving, she was probably coming to get me. I began to take a series of slow, trembling steps until I reached the other side.

She kissed me on the cheek. "See? Nothing to it!"

"Ugh," I replied, rolling my eyes. "My folks are gonna love you."

As we approached the summit, the unthinkable happened. Violet took a step to peer over the edge, and the rock under her foot gave way. Her body lurched forward, and a panicked scream caught in her throat. The ground beneath her crumbled, sending a shower of stones into the canyon below us. For an instant, she was airborne, frozen between life and death.

I instinctively reached out for her, just barely grabbing her backpack. With one hand on the chain and one hand on her, I stopped her slide with a sudden lurch. Her terrified screams echoed off the canyon walls as she flailed her arms and legs, trying to find anything to grab or step onto. My muscles strained to hold on. Summoning every ounce of strength, I gritted my teeth and pulled on her pack, hauling her up over the edge. She collapsed against me, trembling, her breath ragged and shallow.

Silence fell between us as we both caught our breath.

"Are you alright?" I asked cautiously.

She nodded, and then the tears started. Hot, involuntary, repeating sobs spilled out of her. She gripped my arms like a vice, her body still violently trembling. She looked up at me in a storm of emotions as fear, relief, and gratitude muddled together. I hugged her tightly. She buried her face in my shoulder, trying to control her sobbing. After a few minutes, she composed herself and looked up at me.

"You saved my life," she said with an astonished look on her face.

"Yeah, well let's not make a habit of it, alright?"

She giggled, wiping the tears from her cheeks.

"We can turn around if that rattled you too much," I said, trying to comfort her. "If you don't want to finish, I understand. It's just a hike."

A stern look of determination filled her eyes. "No. Now I have to finish. I put my whole life on hold to watch my parents wither and die with regret in their hearts because they chose 'safe' lives. After that, I swore I'd never make choices based on fear. Let's go."

I nodded, impressed again by her resilience. We continued up the trail slowly and carefully. I could tell she was still processing what just happened because her steps became very intentional and deliberate. After about another half hour of climbing, we finally crested the summit. The view from the top was the very best that Zion had to offer. It felt like we could grab the clouds with our bare hands.

Caught up in the victory of finishing arguably one of the harder hikes in North America, I didn't realize how hungry I was. We sat on the plateau area of the summit and ate lunch, greeting fellow hikers that finished the climb as well.

On the way back down, which was no less nerve-wracking than the climb, Violet and I got talking about the relationships in our lives—friends, family, and otherwise. She remarked on how much fun she had with Alicia and Samm. She could see why I was close with the two of them. I asked about her close friends.

"Eh, I don't know if I have any," she replied.

"What?! How is that possible? How can a woman of your caliber not have close friendships?"

She blushed a little. "You're sweet. I mean, I don't have any siblings, dependents, or major responsibilities outside of my job, and I travel a lot. Doesn't leave a lot of time for building relationships. It can get lonely at times. I think all of us crave companionship on some level."

Companionship. It kept resurfacing. Life is not a solo adventure. We really do need each other.

"So, you've never had *any* close friendships?" I asked.

She shrugged. "I wouldn't say *never*. I've still got a few buddies from college that live close by, but we're in different parts of our lives now. They all have spouses and children. That makes it hard to schedule stuff. There was one person, her name was Faith, but things didn't work out."

"Did something happen?"

She shook her head. "No. That's the crazy part. There was no drama, no major event. I just started noticing patterns after a while."

"What do you mean?" I asked.

"Well, it felt like all the effort was one-sided. Everything depended on me reaching out. It felt like our friendship was always on her terms, always on her schedule. I would text her to set something up, and she would always show up late or cancel at the last minute. She would never inconvenience herself for the sake of our friendship, something I did for her constantly. So, one day, I stopped reaching out."

She abruptly went quiet, like that was the end of the story.

"What happened then?" I asked.

She looked up at the cliff walls and sighed. "Complete silence. Sure, we spied on each other's lives through our social media accounts, but she didn't make a single attempt to contact me."

"She just vanished? Like no contact whatsoever?"

Violet shrugged, continuing down the trail. "Nope. Not even on my birthday. It bummed me out more than I like to admit. So, I did a little travel therapy, like usual. I rented a place on the south shore of Hilton Head to do some soul-searching on the beach. After a few days of soaking up the sun and making fists with my toes in the sand, I decided to kick a few bad habits and do some personal development. Figured that at the very least, I could avoid another fake friendship like hers."

We stopped for a quick sip of water from our backpacks, looking out at the deep, time-worn valley and surrounding cliffs.

"I know I'm a bit of a loner, Inertia, but it's what life made me. I know it's off-putting for most people, so to answer your question, no, I don't have a lot of friends." She looked down for a second and then back up at me with a smile. "Don't worry, though. There's at least one special person in my life," she said, hip-checking me.

It was a side of her I hadn't seen yet. Yes, she was tough, resilient, and grounded. Her life experiences had certainly molded her into a self-sufficient and confident person. However, there was a soft, tender version of Violet that longed for companionship as much as I did. We walked the rest of the way back in relative silence, appreciating our surroundings in quiet contemplation. That night, we turned in early, dead tired from the hike.

I climbed into bed, already feeling my muscles starting to tighten. She curled up against me, her warm body pressed against my skin. The gentle rhythm of her breathing matched mine, and our arms and legs enveloped each other like linked puzzle pieces as we drifted off to sleep. There is a wonderful completeness about folding someone into your arms at night. The warmth of their skin, the rising and falling of their breathing. It was steady and tender, a feeling I had sorely missed. My track record with romantic relationships was pretty poor up to this point. Every one of them had failed because I was so focused on my work, but life was very different now.

I woke up the next morning to an empty bed. Fear flashed in my mind. Had it all been a dream? As I sat up quickly in bed, my tired muscles reminded me of the climb the prior day. Every inch of my body ached. Just then, Violet walked in sipping on a green smoothie. She had already showered and dressed.

"Well, look who decided to rejoin the living," she said sarcastically.

"Ugh, how are you not dying right now? I feel like I was thrown down a flight of stairs."

She sat next to me on the bed, rubbing her hand on my chest. "Thanks for not letting me die yesterday and for cuddling with me last night. You're super comfy."

She leaned in and kissed me. Her lips were supple and smooth. She set down her smoothie and embraced me with both arms. We kissed each other tenderly a few more times before she shifted, wincing in pain.

"Sore too?" I asked

She nodded, biting her lower lip. "Epically sore."

"Well, it was a pretty epic day."

After we packed our things, we set off in the direction of a campsite near Lake Powell, known for good stargazing. I decided to detour briefly to Antelope Canyon; the famous slot canyon I'd seen so many times on social media. We were practically driving by it, and I thought it would be a cool pit stop. It was busy, filled with other sightseers, but our tour guide was very knowledgeable and showed us all the best spots.

The thick banks of the curvy sandstone bent around corners, making these narrow passageways that were carved out by water over millions of years. The walls rippled like silk frozen mid-motion, with layers of amber and rose-colored rock. The beams of light that pierced down into the canyon gave me that familiar otherworldly vibe. We walked along in amazement as we moved from light to dark sections, every twist and turn revealing a new sculpture or shadow. It was cool how the light would bend its way into the open spaces, illuminating the sandstone almost like stained glass.

Despite the crowds, it was deeply spiritual, like we were walking on sacred ground. A sense of peace and serenity fell over me as my hand slid across the surfaces of the rock. Everything was new. Potentiality seeped into me with every step through the canyon. It felt like I was shedding the skin of my old life. It was like I was casting off the man that was and becoming someone completely different.

After the tour, we arrived at our campsite for the evening. I started a small fire while Violet set up our tent. My usually busy mind was remarkably quiet. The peace I felt in the canyon began to expand. I smiled, realizing that the gnawing absence in my heart had almost vanished; it was barely a whisper now.

Maybe I did doubt myself too much. Maybe I should accept the good things people say about me. I wasn't the boisterous extrovert or the spontaneous adventurer, but maybe I didn't have to be. Maybe I could just be Inertia Hollins, the easy-to-trust peacekeeper who was a willing ear for the world. Maybe that was enough.

That night, we lay flat on our backs staring up at the night sky. As the warmth of the sandstone faded away, the sky began to transform. It started as a deep indigo and then became a dark canvas of limitlessness. I found myself completely absorbed by an ever-increasing sense of childlike wonderment. I had never seen so many stars in my life. This was impossible to see back home. There was just too much light pollution in the city.

The Milky Way stretched across the sky like a celestial river of light. It was alive and pulsing with shimmering intensity. Dense clusters of stars glimmered like piles of spilled diamonds across black velvet. There were too many to count, each a distant sun, each another world entirely. Our whole journey, we were surrounded by cathedrals of stone, and now we were treated to a cathedral of starlight. It was like every twinkling light in the galaxy showed up to say hello.

While Violet searched the sky for constellations, I reflected on how far I'd come, literally and figuratively, from the man I was prior to Charlie's passing. It had been a little over a year, and I was barely recognizable from my previous self. I thought about how rigidly I held onto my fears back then, reluctant to expose any vulnerabilities. I realized that night, in the audience of the heavens, that was a mistake.

Vulnerability is painful but also necessary. I had allowed myself over this series of trips to share with multiple people the trauma I had experienced, to explore the things I disliked about myself, and to take risks with strangers that had quickly become new friends.

The pain of that vulnerability was the price of the self-worth that now filled my heart. The puzzle was complete. The emptiness had vanished.

That night, I slept soundly, deeply, and free of nightmares. I woke up the next morning feeling fully alive. I had honored my best friend's wishes, broken my own cycle of self-loathing, made a few lifelong friends, and met a wonderful woman that I was quickly realizing I wanted to share the rest of my life with.

CHAPTER FOURTEEN

The Value in the Clay

It was within me all along. Here I had spent so much time searching for something external, looking for that "missing piece" that it seemed everyone else had and I lacked. Except there was no missing piece. Everything I needed, I already possessed. Comparison really is the thief of joy. Violet and Myles were both right—I was already enough.

Things between Violet and me continued to grow increasingly passionate over the months that followed our trip southwest. She got along great with my parents, like I expected. Everything felt right. I loved this woman. There was no denying it. In every version of my future, I saw her face and her mischievous grin. We found a cool apartment through one of Myles's realtor friends and moved in together. Secretly, I started shopping for a ring, wanting to ensure that we could build a life together, but that story will need to wait for another time.

Life entered a season of possibility. However, during my journey, there were many lessons, even if they took time for me to learn. Wisdom can be elusive like that; sometimes, we gain it after we could have used it. When Charlie told me to "just say yes" to the unknown, I did so out of obligation instead of the spirit of adventure. When Myles imparted his rule that "everything is what you make it," I didn't see the power of choice I had in my hands, and it didn't seem applicable for the emptiness in my life at that time.

When Samm said my pain would be "part of someone else's survival guide," it lifted my spirits, but helping others seemed impossible at a time when I was barely helping myself. When Mama J said I would "look forward to the discomfort of unfamiliar things," it sounded crazy because I didn't realize that those unfamiliar things would help me grow, and stretch, and become. When Auggie told me that "the shortcut is a lie," it hurt, because I knew that I had to unwind a lot of heavy feelings on the path to better days. What I didn't see was that dealing with those tough emotions is what *made* those better days.

Then there was Jamala Smith, who feels more like the soul of the forest every time I tell the story, that encouraged me to find the silence and hear the truth it had to tell. A truth that saved me from my guilt and helped me move on. Which eventually led me to my "bruddah" Patrice, who told me that "grief was all the love I never got to share." That it was proof of joy. Then of course there was Violet, who unknowingly rekindled my wanderlust, stole my heart, and made me realize my value in the world.

In retrospect, they were all valuable lessons. Each one I can connect to that sharp-dressed kid with the confident stride and fiery gaze that I met in high school. Were it not for Charlie, I may not have moved to the city, and I may have never met all the wonderful people I now consider chosen family. Equally as true, had I not lost Charlie, I may have never left the city and would have missed out on all the amazing adventures and friendships that happened on the journey.

In a way, losing Charlie helped me *find Inertia.*

∾∾∾

It was Thanksgiving Day. Myles and Julia invited us all up to their place for dinner. My parents had just booked a Rhine River cruise for the spring and were sharing details about the itinerary. Alicia and Samm talked about their upcoming show and surprised us all with tickets.

After the meal, while Myles was cleaning up the kitchen, he asked me to join him for a second. The rest of the crew had retreated to the living room and were laughing and talking around the fireplace. He placed a small stack of legal-sized papers on the table. Julia quietly walked into the kitchen behind him.

"What's that?" I asked.

"Have a look," he said warmly.

Julia placed her hand on my shoulder. "When Charlie's father died so suddenly, my son and I had wills drawn up as a precaution."

She wiped a tear from her eye. "I never imagined I'd outlive them both, but I'm glad we set up safeguards. My son's wishes were simple. In the event of his passing, if he had no spouse or children, most of his assets were to be given to a few charities that were important to him. The rest was to go to you, Inertia. We're sorry it took so long to tell you; the estate planning was more complicated than we expected because of all of Charlie's digital assets. The transfer should only take a day after you sign these documents."

I couldn't believe what I was hearing. Flipping through the pages, I reached the amount. It was enough to live on for a little over a year, maybe more with my own savings. A last gift from Charlie Margolis—*time*. Enough time to figure out what I really loved to do. I could pursue entrepreneurship like Patrice or Fridrik, real estate and philanthropy like Myles, maybe even more travel with Violet—it all seemed within reach.

I hugged them both, shocked and overcome with emotion.

Julia squeezed me back. "Charlie told me many times that you were the anchor in his life, even if he never said those words to you. You were like a brother to him and a second son to me."

⤜⤛⤜⤛

The following Monday, I shared the news with Louis and put in my notice. He was afraid something like that might happen after I tried to quit the last time but shook my hand and wished me well on whatever came next. I didn't hate my job. I had certainly gotten good at it, but it was time to find something that I loved. The office threw me a nice going-away party. Heading home that day, I patted Leonidas on the head one last time.

"Take care, big guy," I said as I pushed the button for the elevator.

As the universe loves irony, I rode down to the lobby with a new hire named Don. He was probably about ten years younger than me, with messy red hair and a crooked tie. He looked exhausted, like I did when I first started.

"How'd your first week go, Don?" I asked him.

"Hard but fun. Lots to learn," he replied with a hopeful smile.

We rode down the rest of the way in silence, stopping at several floors as people got on and off the elevator. Right before we reached the ground floor, I asked him, "So, what do you think of the company?"

He perked up a little. "I like it. Louis seems like a cool boss. Also, the pay is good, and they have great benefits."

I laughed, thinking to myself, *of course he'd say that.*

As the elevator doors opened to the atrium, we headed for the exit. I shook his hand before leaving.

"Good luck, Don."

"Thanks Mr. Hollins."

I nodded. "And Don, *don't be so busy making a living that you forget to build a life.*"

❧❦❧❦

The Park was still.

It was my first day completely unencumbered by the typical obligations of modern life. I had no job to go to, no clients to manage, no traffic and crowds to fight. My time was completely my own. I was sitting on a bench across from the Bethesda Fountain, and the sun was just starting to break over the buildings on Fifth Ave. I wasn't exactly sure what time it was, but it had to be early because an unleashed basset hound wandered over to me and tried to eat my bagel. The dog's owner apologized, but I paid no mind, as my breakfast remained intact. Violet walked over, coffee cups in both hands, and sat next to me.

"Cute dog," she said, handing me a cup.

"Hungry is more like it," I replied.

"So?" Violet's eyes were wide with anticipation. "Today's kind of a big day, right?! You're officially free to do whatever you like? What are you going to do now?"

"Great question, Vee," I said with a big grin. "I have no idea, but I know it'll be awesome."

That was the most honest answer I could manage, and it felt wonderful. A deep sense of peace settled over me. Even if tragedy struck again, I knew I could handle it. I felt like Samm looked that first night I saw her perform—suspended above that crowd, flying along perfectly at ease with her surroundings.

"Well, do you have any ideas?!" Violet asked eagerly.

"Maybe. That journal that Charlie gave me. I've mostly used it for doodles and quotes. Maybe I'll use it for its intended purpose and write the story of my adventures."

She smiled. "Inertia Hollins, the author? Well, that could be cool. You certainly have a good story to tell."

In the months that followed, we did our best to really live each day. Like Charlie did. The second bedroom in our place became an office of sorts. In one corner, I created a place for all the memorabilia from my trips, the centerpiece of which was a selfie Charlie took of us the night he passed. The photo was not there to mourn over but as a reminder to live well.

One evening, while Vee was showering after a run, I sat down in my reading nook (yes, you read that correctly—*my* reading nook) and grabbed my journal. It was weathered a bit from knocking around in my bag through all my travels. I rubbed my thumb over the embossed initials on the cover.

"Hi," I said with a small chuckle. Then, I opened the cover to re-read the note he had left me.

Find yourself. You're the only one who can. – Best, CM3.

I flipped through all the notes and doodles that filled the first dozen pages—thoughts, memories, and bits of wisdom from my travels. I thought about my comment to Violet about writing the story of my adventures. The idea was never far from my mind. It gnawed at me. A whisper of fear entered my head. Who was I to tell any tale? I was no author, no great literary mind. I had no credentials worth noting, no published works of any merit. Who would even care?

I'm happy to report that those thoughts were short-lived, quickly replaced by what I knew in my heart to be true—I was already worthy. I always had been. I may have needed events and people to prove that to myself, but just like Myles had said, "The value was already in the clay."

I was a far cry from that timid boy in high school with the low self-confidence and the strange name. In fact, I had grown into the type of person that would have defended and protected my younger self. The lessons I had learned were worth knowing, and I had a story worth telling.

We all do.

"Begin with the end in mind," Charlie said to me once, quoting some brilliant thinker he had read about. I turned to the next clean page in my journal and did exactly that.

> *Alright, my friend, I've put this off for long enough.*
>
> *I suppose it's time.*
>
> *Thank you for the journal. I think about you every day.*
>
> *My name is Inertia Hollins. Yes, that's my given name ...*

The End
(For now)